T0168355

Fred in Love

Fred in Love

Felice Picano

THE UNIVERSITY OF WISCONSIN PRESS
TERRACE BOOKS

The University of Wisconsin Press
1930 Monroe Street
Madison, Wisconsin 53711

www.wisc.edu/wisconsinpress/

3 Henrietta Street
London WC2E 8LU, England

1   3   5   4   2

Printed in the United States of America

Library of Congress Cataloging-in-Publication Data
Picano, Felice, 1944–
Fred in love / Felice Picano.
p.   cm.
ISBN 0-299-20910-5 (hardcover: alk. paper)
1. Picano, Felice, 1944– .
2. Authors, American—20th century—Biography.
3. Cat owners—United States—Biography.
4. Cats—United States—Anecdotes.   I. Title.
PS3566.I25Z465   2005
813′.54—dc22   2004025623

Terrace Books, a division of the University of Wisconsin Press,
takes its name from the Memorial Union Terrace, located at
the University of Wisconsin–Madison. Since its inception in 1907,
the Wisconsin Union has provided a venue for students, faculty,
staff, and alumni to debate art, music, politics, and the issues of the day.
It is a place where theater, music, drama, dance, outdoor activities, and
major speakers are made available to the campus and the community.
To learn more about the Union, visit www.union.wisc.edu.

For

KAY SALZ

and of course,

FRED

"You're beginning to fascinate me.
And I resent that in any man!"
    Alice Brady to Eric Blore in
        The Gay Divorcee

One

I first became acquainted with Fred as the result of an act of sexual intercourse. A year later, I became more deeply attached to Fred because of a thwarted act of sexual intercourse. And I'm almost certain that I altogether lost Fred, some six years later, because of one or more acts of sexual intercourse.

This might not seem like such a peculiar matter to share in a relationship, until I reveal that Fred was a cat. And no, Fred and I never had intercourse together.

Fred was my second cat of three altogether. Fourth of five if you count the two I grew up with. I guess one has to count them. Them and the cats around myself afterwards, from lovers and pals too. Making him about fourth of seven. That's just the way it happens: cats always end up leaving *some* kind of impression.

Take for example the first cat I recall in my life, elegant Chloe, all black save for tiny white boots on her front paws and a narrow white diamond on her chest. She was my mother's pet. I'm not certain how Chloe came into our lives, but she remained in our house for two years or so, until my father decided she'd be useful at rat-catching at his place of business. Refined, if temperamental, Chloe then reigned over the lower regions of my father's store, well fed and fairly well treated, if less glamorously pampered than before, and while no one ever saw her actually drag a dead—or even a slightly wounded—rodent into view, her presence alone seems to have kept the vermin in line. Or out of sight, which amounts to the same thing.

Partly, this might have been all show. I recall the last time I laid eyes on Chloe: we were in my father's office, she was just outside. Like most cats, she knew she was being spoken of and decided to make herself appear useful. She slinked herself down, pointed her nose and ears forward, and began to vibrate, as though ferreting out something under the woodwork molding. Although she made all the appropriate motions and sounds, Chloe never achieved the climactic leap that would cap her "hunt." Probably because there was nothing to leap at, and after all, she wasn't that foolish. When the rest of us were momentarily distracted by something else, she sat up—act over—to blithely wash her face and head.

At least Chloe knew she was a cat. Our second feline had a far more indistinct sense of what species she belonged to. She'd arrived home one night in a small brown cardboard box, thanks to my father, and she was intended for all of us Picano children. Could she have been the consequence of some indiscretion Chloe had been caught in? we later wondered. But Chloe was a cat we'd always assumed far too exquisite to stoop to mere pregnancy. Whomever the new kitten's parents were, she was delightful and as a result, spoiled beyond belief. What would you expect, a cat being raised by four children and a dog? However, as each Picano child was—to put it kindly—distinctive, this also meant that each of us had peculiar, often directly contrary, notions of how to nurture and treat a pet. As a result, the befuddled kitten chose to imitate none of us, instead taking her clues from—the dog! This concluded with her soon displaying more than one insalubrious inclination, as well as a generally offbeat temperament.

In short, she came to believe she was a dog. She never meowed that I or anyone else ever heard. She ate out of the dog's dish, ignoring cans of fine tuna and cat food to opt instead for filling if crunchy Alpo and those broken dog-bits the sheepdog left. She slept alongside the dog, and like a cur, she simply flopped down anywhere to nap, all over the house, favoring the staircase between our bedrooms and living room, where she'd be sure to be petted or stepped on and abused—again like

3

a housebroken hound. When presented with our hand-made, makeshift, cat box, she abbreviatedly, sniffily, examined it with some interest, but alas, neglected it forever after. All attempts to place and keep her inside its confines resulted in beach sand scattered about our finished knotty-pine basement, bitten fingers, scratched arms, and an alarming increase in the domestic use of four letter words. Instead, Puppy chose to go out, side by side, with the dog, doing what she had to in the yard and even making vaguely appropriate paw motions to cover it over with dirt. The very few times any of us was industrious enough to put the dog on a leash and actually walk it, the kitten followed, and did her business in the street, simultaneously, and in as similar as fashion as she could, although she was clearly peeved to not be able to lift her back leg in any but the most abortive of gestures.

Is it any surprise that we came to call her Puppy? But the worst is yet to come, for the deluded Puppy, unlike our sluggish canine, but like several other nearby dogs, somehow developed a proclivity for chasing cars in our suburban neighborhood. With the anticipated result. Not yet a year old, Puppy was mowed down by an unobservant neighbor's Edsel Suburban. We buried her in our back garden—along with her favorite, surprisingly well-gnawed, bone.

Childhood over, I put aside childhood things—including pets. Until, that is, my roommate, Michael Robinson, moved out of the bargain apartment he and

I (and sometimes his girlfriend too) had shared during our college years on (Far) East 11th Street in Manhattan. Michael had sauntered on to graduate school at the University of Minnesota, while despite faint stabs at an MFA Program in English at Columbia that I never took very seriously, I went to work. The VISTA Program was a Johnson Administration boon, a home-based arm of the Peace Corps set in the ghettos of major cities in America. Because of my presumed knowledge of New York City and my purported skills in Spanish (I'd taken it for what seemed decades in school) I was assigned to render social work in East Harlem. Crazy as the job turned out to be, one advantage was that it was located a single, lengthy, subway ride away from where I lived, and as a result of the work I slowly, eventually came to meet new people and start a new life after my college pals in lower Manhattan—often two at a time—went to grad school, took jobs, married, or just vanished from the scene.

I don't recall exactly how my first solo cat, Gustave, came into my life. I'm now thinking it was through Phillip and Barbara Smuckler, friends from Queens College who lived on East 11th Street and who deposited him with me to "watch a while" when they departed for "restricted" dorm living at one of the more rural campuses of the Pennsylvania State University (restricted in terms of pets: Phil and Barbara lived together). Needless to say, they never again asked after Gustave, and my "watching" became my "living with" him.

Gustave's hypothetical function had been to keep me company and I suppose also to assuage my loneliness, brought on by the defection of just about everyone I knew or had hung out with for the previous four years. All well and good, except that Gustave turned out to be an astronomically uninteresting cat. Tedious, tiresome, boring, dim, torpid, obtuse, prosaic, and pedestrian, Gustave was—to quote Alexander Pope—not only dull himself, he was also the cause of dullness in others. As his "other" was chiefly myself, I soon grew even more downcast, while the apathetic animal proved of no earthly avail. I vaguely recall Gustave's coloring: a sort of walnut, with gray and white markings and bright yellow eyes, not dissimilar from the deluded, self-destructive Puppy.

Of Gustave's personality, I can offer not a suspicion, as in the year or so he lived in my apartment he never offered any evidence whatsoever of possessing such an article. I had around that time become a confirmed, if only barely enthusiastic, Mahlerite, explicating the origin of Gustave's name. If he possessed a former name I can't recall it; and it's a sign of his immeasurable colorlessness that he seemed not to care what I or anyone called him—or even if we did call him. Unlike Fred later on—a Baroque enthusiast with particular penchants for Vivaldi, Leclair, but also the pop artist Nilsson—and despite his musical nomenclature, Gustave showed no definite taste for the music of either his namesake nor for any other composer.

Only in the manner of his leaving was Gustave in any way exciting. I came home from the rigors of social work one fall day to find him foaming at the mouth. I was able to manipulate his flailing limbs inside a zippered gym bag, to get his face wiped and his head sticking out for air, and rushed him to our local vet for an examination. A day later, I was informed that Gustave had developed a brain tumor the size of a Key lime: naturally it was fatal. On the vet's insistence, an hour later Gustave was euthanized.

Once again abandoned, I was left to reflect on what was so wrong with my character that even a dreary pet died on me. A week after his untimely end, I awakened in the middle of the night, hallucinating Gustave out on the airshaft ledge, mewling to get in. . . . These were not my happiest years.

Gustave died in nineteen sixty-six. After the required two years, I quit my job and moved to the West Village then promptly flew off to Europe while friends sublet my apartment. I returned to the U.S. in the fall of Nineteen Sixty Seven and moved into my new studio on Jane Street. In seven months, I would move again, down the street to a small four room apartment, and it would be there, after another some years had passed, that I again had a cat in my life.

In the meanwhile, however, I did have several boyfriends—which, let's face it, is hardly equal to having a good cat in one's life; but then I was young—and once those three or four men proved impossible to remain with, never mind to live with, I managed to develop a medley of casual drop-ins: sex only. During what others have called this "transitional" period of my life, I also had a melange of jobs, one more meaningless and dispiriting than the next. I somehow contrived it so that half of the time I was unemployed; this became, more or less my own choice. I'd usually work for six months, say, freelance filing or cataloguing for some individual or small business. Or I would clerk in a bookstore. Then, once I'd amassed sufficient money, I'd convince them to let me go; or if they balked at that, I'd simply retire and take off the next six months.

The reason behind such a spotty work history is that I was in the extremely precarious process of self-apprenticing myself to become—don't shake your head!—a writer. I desperately needed the free time. And just as much, I needed the mental space provided by being unemployed to become a writer. Often in these years, I found myself so poor I could barely feed myself, never mind a pet. Rent, phone and utility bills were persistently in arrears. I did learn how to cook rice about a hundred different ways, utilizing whatever other comestibles happened to be at hand: meat, greens, vegetables, often just condiments. Despite endless requests and applications for grants, stipends or loans, I succeeded in receiving financial help from absolutely no one, personal or professional. Nine-tenths of those I did hit up—including family—went out of their way to persuade me that I was wasting my time: I would never become a writer, I ought instead to settle down and evolve a career of oblivious, unfulfilling activity, like everyone else in the world. I'd like to note here that the great majority of these ultra-"realistic," unhelpful friends conveniently vanished the day my first novel was published. The few around still waiting for me to fall on my face fled when that book was nominated for a prominent literary award. Those few, intrepid nay-sayers still hanging around (I guess waiting for the axe to fall and my lack of talent to become known far and wide) at last went deep into hiding when my second book became a paperback best-seller. None have come to light since, and I trust that each and every one of them are deeply disturbed, if not actually physically pained, whenever a book of mine is reviewed or is short-listed for yet another award. Even so, had I known it at the time, the financial roller coaster track—mainly conducted far below sea level—that I careened along during that so-called apprentice period ended up being superlative training, allowing me to acquire the steel nerves needed in finances that every writer not blessed with a trust fund has to eventually develop.

When I wasn't worrying where my next meal would come from, Spenserian sonnets, short stories, and novels filled my mind and my life. Whatever left over thought I had went to attractive young men to sleep with and, if expedient, have a bit of romance with. Possibly close to the very bottom of the list of things I considered would be: a cat. That would change as a result of one young man I'd begun to see more regularly.

I'd just been unceremoniously dropped by the lean, handsome star of an early Andy Warhol Studio film who had run off to Californ-eye-ay for a film career (that never got beyond the studio sofa or off the ground) when I encountered Walter. Like my recent dumper, Walter was a midwestern farmboy, redhaired all over. Unlike my dumper, he wasn't an actor, but instead a musician, a composer. Son of a Lutheran minister in a tiny Minnesota town, Walter had learned to read music, play keyboard and sing when he was a toddler. Over the years he'd improved until he was quite good at all of those activities.

Until it was burgled, my Fischer 400 receiver was one of the best music systems around. I had linked it up to a good KLH turntable and a pair of small, ultra-efficient, Acoustic Research speakers. I'd bought the entire set-up during those all too brief, palmy days of regular paychecks but I'd never once regretted its high price, nor the need to occasionally replace its luminous, bulky radio tubes. Walter and I would smoke grass, make love, listen to Mozart's *Prague* or Messiaen's *Turangalila* Symphony or Haydn's *Sun* quartets, enraptured, then smoke more grass and make love again, until we either fell asleep or were driven out of bed by hunger.

When I first met him, Walter lived uptown, on the East Side, but one particular summer he was house-sitting an apartment on Little West 13th Street, only four blocks from Jane Street, where I lived, and as a result we saw each other often. This, despite the fact that he also dated America's most acclaimed, successful young composer of Broadway musicals.

It was one balmy near-autumn evening at this other apartment, following an afternoon of love-making and listening to music, that we glanced out the window and noticed a spectacular sunset over the Hudson River. Walter suggested we go up to the roof to get a better look. There we met a young woman who lived on the same floor as Walter. She had a cardboard box filled with kittens. Her cat had gotten pregnant and she could only keep one of the offspring. She was giving the others away. Could we take one each?

Walter couldn't. He was living from house-sit to house-sit. I also said no. I did look into the box, attracted by one tiny meowing ball of black fur. As I leaned over, another kitten jumped up and attached itself firmly—claws deep—to my pullover sweatshirt. This kitten was pale gray with white markings. Cute and tiny, like the others. About two weeks old, she told us. And it wouldn't let go. Every time I removed one paw, another dug in more deeply. Not deep enough to hurt, just deep enough to remain attached. The kitten seemed to be a male—a fact in its favor. If I were to keep it, it would have to be neutered, a medical procedure I could ill afford. But at least it wouldn't bring home more kittens as a female might. This ball of fur wasn't loudly meowing or particularly needy. It was soft and cuddly and cute and it repeatedly licked my face and nuzzled me.

Walter's neighbor went on to say that those kittens not given away would have to be destroyed. This kitten was obviously doing everything he could not to be one of those left over. The mescaline-induced-looking sunset had turned to starry night, when Walter and I finally stood up to go. I removed the kitten and put it back in the box. It leapt up onto my sweatshirt and crawled behind my neck, where it loudly, claws sunk deeply, refused to be taken off. Both Walter and the young woman insisted that the kitten had chosen me. Not wishing to be regarded as overtly hardhearted, I found that I had no choice but to take the kitten home.

It curled up and slept in my pocket while Walter and I ate at our local hamburger shop, and it was so silent and unmoving I'd all but forgotten the kitten was there in my sweatshirt pocket, until I reached home, walked to my door and was kissed by affectionate Walter. But once he took off and I went indoors I was suddenly faced with the tiny sleeping animal.

Probably because of the musical affiliation by which it had come into my life, I decided to name my tiny new buddy Frescobaldi, after the early Baroque composer, considered to be the earliest and for half a century *the* European keyboard virtuoso. That first night,

Frescobaldi meowed annoyingly loudly outside my closed bedroom door, making sleep impossible. Finally I picked up the little terrycloth towel I had twisted into what I hoped was a cuddly bed, brought it into my bedroom and placed it up on my bed where he could be near me, smell me, and see me. That worked. He stopped meowing and immediately went to sleep.

The same thing happened the next night and the next. Even the one time that Walter slept over, the kitten in his twisted little terrycloth bed insisted upon being brought up onto the bed, between the two of us.

So began a custom that would alter little in years to come. Thereafter, no matter what condition either of us—myself or the cat—was in, no matter who else was staying over, he always had, or managed to force, entry into my bedroom, often attempting to get up on the bed and be within kissing distance of my face. And even when I was most annoyed—"Where have you been? You look terrible! And you smell even worse!"—I always let him.

Two

What also set the pattern of our living together was that aside from needing to sleep by me—or at the foot of the bed—Frescobaldi turned out to be nearly trouble-free, an otherwise perfect pet. He was quiet, frisky, affectionate, quite able to amuse himself for long periods of time, yet lots of fun to watch and play with. He ate readily, at first from the little baby bottle tip Walter's neighbor had supplied, then quickly on his own, diving messily if quite capably into his wet cat food and his dry kitten chow. Never fussy, always interested in trying out new foods; he would sniff at then nibble a bit of spaghetti with a little meat sauce I had dropped into his bowl, eat it up and meow for more. Never shy about what he liked, he ended up nearly omnivorous: he liked all kinds of pasta, cooked spinach, creamed corn, pickled beets, rare green beans, at times even lightly dressed salad. He also nibbled small amounts of yogurt and ice cream and he adored the monthly egg I provided to keep the shine in his coat. No fish or meat entree ever was served in my apartment without a small piece being added to his cat dish. Because he learned to expect a nibble, he never begged from or bothered anyone eating.

Upon closer inspection, he was also one of the prettiest cats I'd ever seen; a real silver gray, and as he got older his white markings accumulated black accentuations, especially on his face, around his eyes, giving him an alert, intelligent appearance which exactly matched his character. On his chest, the narrow whitish center band widened as he grew, achieving thin black stripes against a dove gray background, making him look like a gray cat wearing an old fashioned French tennis shirt.

What became even more clear to me—who'd never raised an animal all by myself—was that Frescobaldi wasn't that different from a little human boy. His education was easy for the most part because he was so smart and because he wanted to please me. He learned to ask for what he liked, quickly discovered how to use his cat box—and later on, learned to go outside, meaning I need not even *keep* a cat box. He quickly figured out what *not* to play with in the house—electrical wiring for instance. Then again, like any other toddler, at times he would want his own way and become fixated upon getting it.

Which was how we arrived at the moment where Frescobaldi had grown big enough to jump up on my writing desk. He was still quite small. Maybe seven weeks old, but he was actively testing his athletic and coordination skills upon pretty much every piece of furniture and object in the apartment. Fine. For the most part I let him. I had few breakable things, and even less of any real value to be grieved over *if* broken.

He'd already come to understand that he and I ate separately, on two levels, he out of his cat dish on the floor, me on the table. But one day when I sat down at my desk to do some writing, Frescobaldi leapt up. I said no, and put him down on the floor. He leapt up again. He must have thought—because it was clear by this juncture that he did actually think in some fashion— that I was at the desk hours at a time, and therefore *something* interesting must be happening up there. He had no clue what, but he was determined to find out.

I let him sit a minute up on the desktop, showing him what I was doing, in this case, writing in my journal. He sniffed around a bit and watched me. When he became disinterested, I gently picked him up and put him down on the floor.

He jumped up again. Again I lifted him down saying no gently, handling him gently. He jumped up again. I put him down again. And again. I began to count how many times this happened. I was oddly calm, not in any way annoyed. Still when the count reached twenty and he was still leaping up and I was still gently saying no and placing him back on the floor, I wondered why he—so quick at picking up other things—wasn't grasping this, simple as it was, similar as it was to the situation with the dining room table, which he'd easily learned.

I tried again and again. We reached thirty times. At which point I supposed this wasn't a case of not understanding at all. This little problem somehow stood for everything else in our relationship: he the pet, me the person; he the learner, me the teacher. (I almost added he the owned, me the owner; except everyone knows you never *own* a cat.) We'd reached forty times now, although a longer time elapsed between each leap up, and he would remain grooming himself nervously before once more jumping up. Fifty times.

I wondered how high we would go. At fifty-three he hesitated, and I looked down and warned, "No-oo! No jumping up on this desk. Anywhere else but this desk." He jumped again anyway and I once more said no and placed him down on the floor. Fifty-four. Fifty-five. Then he stopped. Simply turned around and went to his water bowl. I sat calmly at the desk. All thoughts of writing had already long vanished. We were clearly in "cat-training" mode, this afternoon.

Twice more, Frescobaldi approached the desk. One he looked up and made as though to jump. But when I warned him off, he instead groomed himself. Another time, some five minutes later, he sat there and meowed at me for a good two minutes, in what I'd begun to recognize as his questioning tone of voice, as all the while I warned him off.

He was telling me he didn't understand why he couldn't be up on my desk. I was responding that I didn't care if he understood me or not, he had to stay off. Ten minutes later, he was gone from the room, and I started to work. In all the years to come, he never once leapt on that writing desk. I could put anything there: a burning candle, a magazine cover with marijuana I was cleaning and getting ready to roll, my glasses, anything at all, with no fear at all that he would upset it. It proved to be a valuable lesson for the two of us. We'd started to learn to live together as two distinct individuals.

Three

What I hadn't grasped at the time of the desk incident was that if I was training my kitten, he was also training me. Learning to live together is a two-way street, and while other animals in the home eventually acquiesce to human bullying, cats can be far smarter and slier. They also have specific, often contrary, opinions about things, and if they are persistent, you can one day turn around and discover you are both doing it their way, and not yours.

Clearly, however, Frescobaldi was a benevolent dictator and so the foremost way in which he would train me was in the arena of affection.

By my mid-twenties I was emotionally at the edge of what Graham Greene had so aptly, even felicitously, called, a burnt-out case. I'd already gone through several major separations of people in my life: first, in my teens, my family and those I'd grown up with when I'd moved out of my parent's house and ended contact with them; second, by twenty, my later high school and college pals when we'd all graduated and they had all moved away; third, at twenty-five, the group of pals I'd made working in Spanish Harlem whom I no longer saw now that I'd left that job. Since then, I'd seldom stayed at any job long enough to make friends in this era. I had been to Europe, and I had gone through one fun group of pals in Rome, and another, less intimate one in London. Back in New York, living in Manhattan's Greenwich Village I was very slowly, very warily, sidling back into "society" via my association with a loosely knit group of gay men—and a sprinkling of women—who lived in or around the same tenement building, who I would stick with for a few more years. I would later come to call them the Jane Street Girls.

Even the most superficial glance around myself revealed that my personal life, marked by separations, misunderstandings, and flubbed opportunities, was neither ordinary nor very successful. I knew people three times my age who still associated with their families and those they'd grown up with; I knew a lot more people whose lives had expanded to include high school and college friends. Meanwhile I had no relationships with the women I used to know, although some had been close; having persuaded myself that since I was homosexual, what was the sense. But once having accepted myself as a gay man, I'd then been involved in several romantic disasters in a row; so I'd also come to avoid any male-on-male relationship I happened to find myself in. That is, except, when their radar was better than mine and they managed to get away from me first.

How deeply alienated, doubtful and suspicious of any other human I'd become around the time Frescobaldi entered my life was forcefully pointed out to me one time when visiting my parents for Sunday dinner — a trek to the suburbs involving three changes of subway and a lengthy city bus ride, a two hour minimum going either direction. I was standing in the kitchen talking to my mother, and she lifted something to my mouth for me to eat. I stopped her hand to look at what exactly was in her hand. "I'm your mother!" she objected. "Do you think I'm going to poison you?!"

At the time, I laughed it off with some lame excuse. But the truth was I already felt poisoned by pretty much everyone I'd associated with since birth. I was depressed about my present life, and worse, could perceive no future worth making any effort for. I found little in life to please me, and often contemplated ending it. Only the shattered remnants of my vanity (still so strong that like a first magnitude star, it could bend light — or in this case, judgment) and my intense need to make a huge splash as I went down in flames actually kept me from killing myself. But I either couldn't imagine how to go out grandly enough; or if I could, I simply couldn't afford to go in the style I thought I deserved.

This was the profoundly despondent existence into which a two week old kitten thrust himself. The naive forcefulness of such an act—since it was as obvious to me as it had been to his mother's owner and to Walter that this kitten had insisted upon being adopted—stopped me. First, I had to deal with the kitten's incessant demands to be cared for. He was, after all, not yet weaned. That mothering was doubled by his incessant demands to be petted, entertained, and in every way not only acknowledged but made much of. These were requirements made upon a young man who by that point could barely bring himself to acknowledge other people, and then usually only to fulfill sexual gratification.

Frescobaldi didn't know from being depressed, therefore not only was he not depressed, but he wouldn't let me be depressed around him. He was young and life was intensely interesting to him. So having a poor attitude wasn't ever an option. It was not included in his schedule of being a kitten, having fun, and growing up. As a result, grumpy me, crabby me, ill-natured, cantankerous, irritable me was forced to . . . play with a kitten! To be nuzzled by a kitten. To have a kitten fall asleep on my lap while I was in an armchair reading. To allow myself to be distracted by a kitten having trouble negotiating a path around the various cans, tins, glass jars, wooden spoons, and metal implements on a kitchen shelf as I cooked, each one of which must be sniffed, inspected, touched, somehow gotten around.

What got me really intrigued was not only observing this fresh new being in his first contact with various aspects of the world, although that was an important element, and might actually be a good reason why people like having infants and toddlers around. Fun as that was, more fascinating by far was watching a new intelligence develop. As I said before, the kitten was vocal, interrogative, from an early age. But more than vocal, Frescobaldi was *manual*. From a very early age he used his paws a great deal to handle the world, something I'd never noticed in a cat before.

He would come upon some object and inspect it, sniff it, then paw at it, first with one foot, then with the other foot. If, like a ball or beetle, the object happened to move at that point, he would jump back a bit, but immediately touch it again to see again how it reacted. He learned to manipulate small objects with his paws, not just one paw at a time, but using two paws. I'd never witnessed this behavior in a cat before. And if the object did something unexpected and totally upsetting, he would back up on his legs and try swatting at it, and when that failed, just wave his paws at it. This was not only innate in him, it also became reinforced, learned behavior.

I wouldn't let him back off in confusion with some recalcitrant object, but would keep him playing with the thing until he could see his effect upon it, become comfortable with it, even at times master the object. I began to notice that he would place himself where he could watch me manipulating objects: cooking, typing, shuffling cards. He'd move in close to me and put a tiny paw upon my hand or finger and meow as though asking me something. I would then explain what I was doing and usually add that cats didn't do this activity very well.

In this manner Frescobaldi began to model those aspects of his behavior that he could copy from my own. Later on, when he was grown, this would mean complex behavior such as standing up on his back legs as though walking and using his paws to turn door handles between rooms, letting himself in and out. He also observed me on the toilet, and in time, he taught himself how to sit on the toilet; although alas he never learned to flush, which I tried to show him.

I would watch him doing cat things—fighting with shadows on the wall, going after objects being moved by a breeze—and I would encourage him in his play behavior. Any half-rolled sock in my bedroom quickly became a hunted object, and once he learned not to be afraid of a pink rubber Spalding ball, he began going after that too.

So he was cute and he was intelligent.

He was also totally dependant upon me for the first six months of his life—unlike my previous cat, Gustave, who for the most part barely knew I existed. Whenever I came home and opened my apartment door, Frescobaldi would run from wherever he'd been and would leap up to greet me with pawings and meows, insisting I pick him up and cuddle him. Whenever I was in the dumps myself, lying motionless, thoughtless on my bed, he would leap up and nuzzle me, push his head into my face, insist upon being petted, and played with, distracting me from my despondency.

The first time I got sick around him, Frescobaldi must have been about four months old: a toddler's age. I'd developed some kind of violent, seventy-two-hour stomach virus and I was moaning and groaning and feverish. At first, Frescobaldi tried pretending that all was as before. When that failed, he was obviously baffled, unsure how to relate to me. He sat watching me from the bedroom floor and I could all but hear him wondering whatever was I doing lying in bed all day when there were so many groovy things to do. Moreover, why was I making those peculiar sounds? They weren't talking to him, nor talking on the phone. What was their purpose? How should he react? He observed from his floor perch for a longish time.

Finally, I'm supposing now as I did then that between my weakened, vulnerable tone of voice and my unusual behavior, he somehow gathered that something was wrong, and he made a decision. Also, amazingly, he seemed to sense that I could use comforting. So he remained in my bedroom, only leaving to drink water and eat dry cat food. Once when the phone rang in the living room and I didn't answer it, he went out into the little hallway and looked back and forth from the ringing phone to me as though asking, "Well? Aren't you going to get it?"

A day later I felt well enough to invite him onto my bed briefly, where he licked my face, groomed and nuzzled me. And when, two days later, I felt much better, got out of bed and began moving around the house again, he was no longer the silent, barely moving, watchful kitten he'd turned himself into. Instead he was himself again, active and playful. Later on I realized that this incident developed a bond between us. I felt—whether foolishly anthropomorphizing or not—that he thought of me as more than that oversized creature who fed and played with him.

After that illness, Frescobladi had as good a sense of me, my moods, my health, as I needed. Even years later, when he was gone days at a time, we would retain this near-telepathic link.

Four

When he was a year and a half old, what would be around ten in cat years, and almost fully grown, Frescobaldi renamed himself. This came about in a very circuitous manner.

When I first got him, I'd not had him neutered, mostly because I couldn't afford to. Of course, I also had other misgivings. The procedure was, to begin with, unnatural. It was extremely invasive surgery. I certainly wouldn't want it done to me. And those "fixed" cats I'd seen, tended to get big and fat around the middle; resembling lino-tints of eighteenth-century "neutered" men—the *Castrati*. Neutered cats had always seemed to me sluggish, they sat around the house all day, not doing much of anything. Nor did they show much interest in things. In other words, *they* no longer seemed natural. Any time the subject of neutering my kitten came up I would feel queasy; especially when it was brought up by my former boyfriend and now upstairs neighbor, Bob Herron, who would usually declare in a tone of voice that brooked not even a glimmer of opposition, "Naturally, you'll have the kitten fixed." I merely nodded or performed some body gesture that he might interpret as assent, by which sign I felt I was making far less of a commitment.

Within the year, however, my income actually rose a bit and so I could have afforded to have the procedure done, had I really wanted to. Obviously I didn't. Which meant that my convictions were more resolute than my sense of duty to my neighbors.

Or was it rather because I had begun to identify with the kitten? I lived on the first floor and during clement weather, as he'd grown, the kitten had begun to sit on the sill in the study or living room whenever the windows were open, sometimes sitting outside a few inches upon an adjoining brickwork ledge. These perches had given the seven-month-old a view of the backyard. Nothing much to speak of, just a fenced in dirt rectangle with a half dozen weedy plants, mostly acacia, a glorified weed which seemed to flourish in Manhattan with no aid, burgeoning into trees during mild winters and temperate spring and summers.

My building's back lot was one of a dozen and a half attached, enclosed yards, each belonging to a neighboring apartment building or brownstone, all of them together spanning the interior length and breadth of the small Greenwich Village block. While I'd never really noticed the backyards—my flat's back windows were so very grimy, even with sporadic efforts at washing them, and the yards were, after all, extraordinarily dingy—Frescobaldi *had* checked them out quite carefully, and among other things, he had noticed others of his species in those rectangles. Plenty of them.

Soon, whenever I'd look out on the ledge to call him back inside, he'd be gone altogether. During that first late spring and summer he lived with me, I took to leaving one window ajar for him to come and go. He always returned home to eat, to sleep, to hang around. He would announce his arrival home with a series of meows as he entered, go to drink out of his water dish, then come to wherever I was, nuzzle me, eagerly, if usually incomprehensibly, narrate what had occurred outside. Often, he would arrive home with minuscule indications of having been around, a spot of dirt here, a few dried leaves stuck in his fur.

I was, during this period, not dating much. Walter had moved back uptown and as I almost never saw him, I supposed he was seeing someone else, probably that Broadway composer, who he told me he found "fascinating if weird." No one else I'd met since interested me enough to call back after a one-night stand. Still, I was in my mid-twenties, restless, and so I'd sometimes find myself out of doors after I'd worked all day and had dinner, doing what others—my neighbor Bob and a floor above him, Kenny—insisted upon calling "catting around."

In truth, during those walks of what were in those years the very sparsely populated night time West Village streets, I was far less interested in finding someone to take home, as they assumed, as I was in simply looking around the neighborhood, checking out buildings, streets, the entire layout of an eighteenth- and nineteenth-century area that had gracefully made the transition into late twentieth century. True, I would sometimes drop into a local bars for a beer. But I seldom spoke to anyone but the bartender. Far less frequently, I'd walk uptown to the first Chelsea-area gay bars opening on West Street in the Lower Twenties.

More often, I'd walk the post-midnight streets of the West Village just to burn off energy, to tire my body enough for sleep, wondering if I'd catch a glimpse of Alexander Hamilton's ghost, as one of my neighbors claimed to have done. The famous Federalist had reportedly been rowed across the Hudson River at night, after being mortally wounded by Aaron Burr. He'd allegedly landed at a dock at the end of Jane Street, and died in a house not far away, an edifice still standing, between Washington Street and the West Side Highway.

Other times, whenever I felt lonely or couldn't get to sleep, I would sit outside my apartment building, perched upon one arm of the concrete stoop—a tiny entrance balcony to my building—with my back against the brown building facade, my legs drawn up to my knees, watching people meander home from parties, or bars, or late night encounters. When Frescobaldi was still small enough, I'd sometimes hold him in my lap while outside. Every once in a while, I would meet someone walking along the uneven, cobblestone streets, or find myself in conversation with someone passing. Not often, but enough to keep from feeling completely isolated.

I reasoned that if I could do that, why shouldn't my cat enjoy the same freedom, the same privilege? In fact, once he was big enough to defend himself I was *glad* he was getting out and sincerely hoped he was meeting other cats, maybe even female ones. He might still be too young for sex during that first year, but he was growing fast. And he was big enough to make other cats notice him. More than once, directly after what sounded like the very loud prelude to a cat fight somewhere in the one of the many backyards, he dashed into my study window. One time he arrived home with a tiny nip bitten out of one young ear, which couldn't have hurt as much as his pride. I managed to smear hydrogen peroxide on it to prevent infection, without him getting too annoyed with me.

Despite how cavalierly he acted about that injury, I noticed that for the next several days he remained indoors, never very far from me. For a few days, he didn't jump up onto the backyard ledge, stayed indoors. That night, when I went to close the study window, I couldn't help but observe a huge, sickly-yellow tomcat outside, his head and face garlanded by nicks and scars of various lengths and depths, visible even from a dozen feet away. He sat there apparently disinterested, washing his face, sniffing the ground.

The tom may have fooled himself that he was acting inconspicuous, but once I'd shut the window and pulled back what passed for a curtain, I noticed him sit up at attention, all pretense of innocence suddenly wiped off his deceptive face, and when I lifted my cat to the window and asked if that's who had nicked his ear, Frescobaldi uncharacteristically squirmed out of my hands and leapt down to the floor. He hid where I couldn't get at him the rest of the night, and even a piece of chicken held out didn't lure him out.

The big tom was there again the next day as I was watering the lone, dispirited philodrendron that passed for green ornamentation in my flat. I yelled at the tom to scram, but it wouldn't flinch, until—angered by its assault on my pet—I hurled the remaining water at it, causing it to yowl and dash under the fence. I never saw it again.

A few days later, Frescobaldi got his courage back and ventured outdoors again, first onto the window sill, then onto the ledge for hours at a time. After a short time, he was gone all day again.

Once autumn began and temperatures began dropping, I tried calling Frescobaldi inside at night so I could shut the window. When he didn't respond (where could he be? he always came to my voice) I tried leaving the window open an inch. He usually managed to meow loudly enough through that open slit to make himself known to me, and I'd get up in the middle of the night and let him in. When it got too cold for even that slit of open window to stay open, I closed it tight, and he took to tapping at the window, which awakened me.

This was made easier because in those days whenever I was home, I wasn't that far from this window. I had another roommate, my first since the days of the ill-fated Bobby Brown. This was another Bob: Chisholm, from Buena Vista, Virgnia, a sweet, smart, good-looking young man who'd studied art at the University of Virginia, from which he'd just graduated, and who'd moved to New York to try his hand at the art world.

Later on Bob would become the owner/operator along with his life partner of the Chisholm Pratt Gallery in Chlesea, which quickly became and still is one of the most important venues for poster art in New York. At that time, he was still looking for work, and love, while sharing my apartment and my rent, and thus increasing my income. When he was home, which became suddenly far less often that summer, Bob Chisholm slept in the little formal bedroom, with its closeable door, while I moved my bed to what had been the dining room/study, a doorless room, equally small, placed catty-corner between the kitchen and living room.

To fit my bed in, I'd moved the gate-leg dining room table out of that room and into the living room, placing it against the wall-long church pew that a pal and I had discovered being given away on the street one Saturday afternoon and had dragged home with enormous effort. The pew was one of the few surviving pieces of furniture from a freshly bombed out Presbyterian church on Perry Street—a crime never to my knowledge solved. Fifteen feet long, the length of my living room's longest solid wall, with a wide, well worn seat, it was made of walnut, almost six feet high, undecorated and very handsome. With a few flat pillows it was comfortable seating. With more pillows and a quilt, it doubled as a narrow bed whenever Bob or I had a guest.

The teakwood gate-leg table, which I'd bought from a friend moving west just before I'd lost my last job, I now placed against the middle of the church pew, and with the table usually folded down on two sides, it created a nice breakfast spot, or impromptu desk for Bob. When it was unfolded, I'd bring my desk chair and another chair, and the dining oval could hold six for dinner.

I had given my kitten the fanciful Sixties name ("Peace! Love! Man!") Frescobaldi. Once he began going out, living much of his time outside, coming in only to eat and sleep, at other times to flop down to rest from the many labors of being a young cat in the city, it was clear he had earned another, different name.

For a while he became "The Junior High School Cat." Then I shortened his name to Fred. After all, he was no longer the all-eyes, button-nosed, fuzz-ball kitten. He was big and handsome—and masculine. He looked like a Fred; and while still a dear, let's face it, he acted klutzy, just like a Fred might. Moreover, when I called him by the name Fred, he responded to it.

In years to come, I would meet and even come to know the miscellaneous cat ladies of my West Village neighborhood, which was still a bohemian district, where—oh days long gone!—you could live cheaply, in small, old, rent-controlled, long-unrenovated digs.

The part of Grenwich Village west of Eighth Avenue and Hudson Street was no longer an immigrant—predominantly Irish American—neighborhood as it had been since around nineteen twenty. But it was still a decade away from being the desirable center for yuppies needing townhouses and duplexes at a not-too-costly cab ride from Wall Street or Madison Avenue. That was what would eventually happen to the area by the mid-Eighties. Even later it would become a funky-glam-downtown-fashion center, with Todd Oldham, Barneys, and Armani F/X shops on narrow, broken-curbed streets that had not very long before been trawled by drag hookers, leather queens and thin, aging uptown socialites delightedly slumming. By the turn of the twenty-first century the West Village was totally transformed from "Beat-Me Fuck-Me country" into "Fab Trash-ville." But by then I'd become an exile, burnt-out by AIDS deaths, driven out by excruciatingly high rent, relocated to the relatively peaceful, beneficent Hollywood Hills—inhabited, alas, by underfed coyotes and hawks, for whom a housecat was a snack, akin to a large burrito.

Those Sixties and Seventies West Village women all seemed to be characters of one sort or another, most of them originally connected with "the Arts," even if only by virtue of being married to or related to others active or actively pretending to be musicians, artists and poets. Not one woman in the group was under fifty years old: the average age was seventy. One dowager was so old she looked downright immortal, and I later learned of her passing with astonishment.

It was through these women that I discovered that my little buddy, Fred, was not only *not* unknown, but that he was prominent among their set. This shouldn't have been any real surprise, as he was a gregarious, attractive animal. Still I found myself somewhat disheartened to perceive that over the past few months he'd regularly visited several ladies up on their second-, third-, even sixth-floor balconies or fire escapes, staying hours at a time—while I'd assumed he was outside having feline adventures. I was even more surprised that he was known to them so personally—fed, petted by all—that he had managed to amass a bunch of aliases.

My first hint of this was the time I bumped into Mizz Chavis-Wilson, who I found out lived on the other side of the backyard, in an interior facing apartment off Horatio Street. When I first came upon her, Mizz Chavis-Wilson was in the process of taping a sign with a blurry looking photo of a missing house cat onto a street light pole, not far from my apartment building. When I stopped to look at it, she turned and asked, "How's Scotty?" She must have been in her late seventies, and had obviously once been a Greenwich Village Bohemian, as she still dressed like a Thirties radical, with colorful, multiple skirts wrapped around her waist, an embroidered vest-like top, hair pulled severely back in a bun, off her handsome if discolored face, graced with granny glasses, and always wearing tiny, highly polished shoes. "Scotty," she repeated. "at least that's what I call him. I see him going into your apartment window all the time."

"Oh you mean my cat, Fred."

"Freddie, is it?" she asked, and began talking about him. It turned out she fed Fred, and when my window was closed, he'd visited her hours at a time. "He's a nice little Freddie," she said. "Smart too. You can teach him things!"

Amused, I answered back, "Algebra?"

She frowned and fussed. "Oh, you young people!"

When I asked Mizz Chavis-Wilson about the big tomcat, she pondered a minute, and shaking her head declared, "Yellow, huh? Well, he's not from this block." Which could only mean that she believed she knew all the cats on the block. "Oh! I know who you mean! Sandy! The mouser! It must be him. A working cat. At the Eclair Bakery."

The bakery was over a block away, on Jane and Greenwich Streets.

"But how does he get into my—our—backyard?" I asked.

"Oh, easily! They all just come and go as they please," she said, surprised at my question. "That's what it means to be an alley cat."

That made me wonder. Had my precious Frescobaldi also turned into an alley cat? One tormented by a wicked mouser, a basely ignoble working-class cat? If so, it meant that the healthy, natural, almost edenic life I'd intended for my kitten to inhabit had turned out instead to be the opposite: a nightmarish street-war inferno.

I tried explaining my qualms to her, but Mizz Chavis-Wilson brushed my concerns aside. "It's too late. And any way, Freddie's smart. He can take care of himself. Your job is to be his daddy," she added, which came out sounding very odd in her prim, New England accent. Then, as she thrashed off to the next street light to hang another sign, she added. "Teach him! Freddie wants to learn!"

Scotty, Freddie, Silver Ears, Silver Dollar, Junior: it later turned out Fred was notorious all over the neighborhood by the ladies who doted on cats. He'd become a local celebrity.

At the end of that first summer, Fred began visiting a newer, a closer neighbor, and although we would probably have met sooner or later, it was through Fred that first I met her. My building was one of two attached, five-story-high brownstones with connected stoops. Employing the same ground plan, they had identical layouts: two slender, long, railroad-style apartments in the front, and a larger, square apartment in the rear of each floor.

Sometime after I'd moved to forty-three Jane Street, through my actor friend George, I met a pal of his, a British actor a few years older who lived in the identical apartment next door. Neville was on the road periodically and I seldom saw him coming or going, but one day during Fred's first year, he rang my bell to visit.

He would be away from home all summer, Neville announced, since the Canadian Royal Academy of Drama he'd recently joined was touring that country, and after it parts of India, all summer. However, an old friend from his student days at R.A.D.A. (i.e., in London) would be visiting from the U.K. and staying in his apartment. I needn't worry if I heard her rattling about inside there. Also, she might require me to help her sometime, he added, although not very much, he thought, as she was rather independent—when that is she wasn't downright headstrong. At any rate, Neville had taken the liberty of giving her my phone number in case of emergency. Was that all right? I said it was fine. Neville seemed pleased as he took off, headed to Yellow Knife and Bangladore and I never gave the matter further thought.

A few weeks later, I heard a woman's voice singing out the back window and I supposed Neville's houseguest had arrived. One time I thought I saw her for an instant shaking out a dust mop. It wasn't easy to make out her face through all that dust and all that reddish hair. Then, a month later, I noticed Fred sitting on her window sill, being petted by a slender, be-ringed hand. "If he's bothering you, just shoo him away!" I said, by way of announcing my presence. Her kerchiefed head barely made it outside to check me out, and because of the sharply angled afternoon light, all I could make out of her was a lot of moiré silk, within which I could descry shadow surrounding a pair of large gray eyes.

"He's a dear, isn't he?" she said in a very British accent. "But are you Neville's friend? Actually, I was planning to ring you up." she said.

I asked why and she said because the flat's corridor lightbulb had gone out and she couldn't reach up to change it. I said I'd come right over.

Neville's apartment, which I'd never been in before, had the identical layout to mine, and was similarly furnished, except he had no church pew in the living room, and instead possessed much Eastern regalia of a quality substantially higher than our local bamboo screen and tatami shop carried: wall-hung Turkish carpets, enormous brass salvers—doubtless from previous touring company trips.

His houseguest turned out to be a tall, somewhat gawky woman, wearing a dark floral housedress with a cotton sweater around her shoulders, buttoned at her throat. She was maybe thirty and very attractive; also, she was somewhat familiar looking, although I couldn't place why. What one instantly noticed about her was that she was pregnant. Extremely, almost ostentatiously, pregnant.

And there my cat, Fred, sat, enthroned upon the seat of Neville's rocking chair, atop pillows covered in Balinese batik, comfortable as he could be, purring away throughout our little encounter, occasionally narrowing his eyes at us in benevolence.

She showed me a small folding ladder, which I put aside as insufficiently tall. Instead I did what I did at home and pulled out a kitchen chair, covered with newspaper, and even then, as at my flat, I had to really stretch up on tip-toe to reach the light bulb dangling so high above in the little hallway. After much effort, at last, the bulb was changed, the switch turned on, and proved to work.

She asked me to sit a minute and offered me tea, which I declined, and a glass of water, which I accepted. We talked at first about the Village, and America, which she didn't know at all well, and about our mutual acquaintance, whom she apparently had known from long before. Once we were comfortably speaking, I asked when she was expecting and if she planned to return to London to give birth.

She was expecting in three months, and she said she would remain in Neville's apartment for the birth, as she was liable to be arrested and gaoled under some archaic British law having to do with a legal charge of adultery, because the child's father was married to someone else. That was why she'd come to the U.S. in the first place, she explained, and why she was hiding and why her presence must be kept hush-hush. As she spoke I suddenly realized why she looked familiar: she was a quite famous film and stage actress, star of both chic foreign language movies and several big-budget Hollywood films that I'd seen and admired.

I tried not to gag on my water at this moment of recognition, and I more or less succeeded in keeping my cool. But my inbred scandal-sensor intuited a story beyond what was being told me, and when I got up the nerve to ask who the father of her baby was, and she answered, I'm afraid I simply lost it, spluttering liquid all over myself.

I'd lived in London's West End a few years before and had read the gossipy *Queen* magazine weekly, and had gotten around Earls Court enough to be up to date on all the rumor, scandal, calumny, and dish. So it just came out of me: "But isn't he the biggest fag on the West End?"

Cascades of laughter came out of her mouth. "He is, isn't he?" she finally admitted. "Still! He's the father of this baby. And of other babies too, unfortunately, Which is why his crazed wife wants me imprisoned! Oh, and by the way, we call them poufters. It's somehow less derogatory."

The buzzer rang: someone had come to visit. I assured her she might rely on my complete silence and she might phone me for anything else she needed, and I lifted up Fred to go home.

She did phone once more that summer; a rather bulky steamer chest had been delivered to her, and she needed help dragging it up the stoop steps and inside to the flat. The chest turned out to be filled with beautiful old chinaware, wrapped in British tabloids with headlines—including several absolutely daffy ones about her—that we giggled over. "Neville's a dear," she explained, as she set up the lovely porcelain, "But his dining service is what one might be forced to use at Borstal, or worse, in some public school's fourth form."

Aside from that incident, I didn't see or hear from her again until the fall, except whenever Fred visited her. Over the next several weeks, however, I did come upon friends of hers, usually because they were waiting for her on the stoop next door. Realizing who they were—i.e., other famous actors—I would help them ring her bell, or confirm that she was not home. One afternoon I returned home to find that a tall, striking fellow had mistakenly written my building number down instead of hers, had rung my bell, and as I wasn't in, was waiting on my stoop. We quickly established whom he was indeed visiting, that she lived next door, that I knew her and he might phone to see if she was currently at home. I offered my phone inside and we began flirting. One thing led to another, so I invited him to stay for tea, which I never got around to brewing, because by then we were too busy removing each other's clothing to get at each others bodies. Never once, during lovemaking nor afterwards, as we lay exhausted in bed smoking cigarettes, did he in any way resemble the character he was famous for playing: Norman Bates.

Then the summer was over, the autumn nearly so, it was nearly Halloween, and Neville had come back triumphant from his tour and moved back in with the actress and he phoned me one late morning totally panicked, "Her water's broken, come help me get her to the hospital."

He was crazed, but she was calm, as I ran to the corner and flagged down a taxi, then as we finagled her along the long hallway and down the steps, oh so slowly, twisting her up and into the backseat of the roomy Checker cab I'd located, Neville a study in untidiness, she neat and contained, busily calming him, as they drove off.

A few weeks later, when I saw Neville checking his mail, I asked after his houseguest and was told that her gay beau had arranged to get the charges against her dropped; and that after Natasha was born, he had flown to New York and brought them back to London, where they were all staying together—at least for the moment. Neville seemed completely fed up with the entire affair, and testily added, "Oh, and by the way, would you mind keeping your cat away from my window sill. He comes in whenever it's open and it turns out I'm horribly allergic."

I told him to just push Fred away the next time he came near.

Winter came and it turned out to be an uncommonly harsh one. Snow began to fall in late November, and by late February, mountains of dirty, multicolored, frozen and refrozen, rock hard snow were still piled up alongside every large and small West Village street. Fred naturally stayed indoors more often. But as soon as the spring arrived, he was clamoring to get out of doors.

He had begun to spray territorially inside the house, and for the very first time in our relationship, he and I had come into minor conflict over his spraying. Once while I was sitting in meditation on the living room floor, I watched Fred enter via his usual path of the study window, walk past me to eat and drink in the kitchen, come back into the living room, sidle around me as I sat in lotus position, nuzzle me outrageously and receive no response at all.

Clearly surprised, he stood in front of me and checked me out a long while, my body absolutely still, my hands crossed in my lap, my breathing shallow and slow, my eyes so closed they were merely strips. After a while, I could tell Fred had convinced himself that I wasn't conscious. He immediately lifted one leg attempting to spray a corner of the living room. I shot out a hand to tap him on the head.

Thunderstruck, Fred turned and fixed me with a look of such surprise and yes, I have to say it, such a look of betrayal—after all, I was supposed to be asleep!

I shouldn't be able to see what he was doing!—that I burst out laughing. I scrambled up to try to gather him up in my arms, and comfort him. But Fred was still furious with me, he wouldn't allow it. He squirmed away from me and shot back out the window.

After that incident, I tried to let Fred out early in the day, and I would leave him outside as long as he wanted. Sometimes, I wouldn't see him for days at a time. Like any other teenager, he now came home when he wanted to, usually just to eat and to sleep. Whenever I tried to pet him or brush his fur, he barely allowed me to before he would get antsy or irritated with me, squirm out of my arms and stalk off. I found myself missing the lovable kitten he'd been, the little thing relying on me for everything. But I consoled myself that at least Fred was leading as normal a life as a house cat could in a city. And along with that came the realization that when I went back to a regular job again, I probably would see him even less often.

It was at precisely that moment that Fred met Jennie, and had his first taste of romance—and a broken heart.

Five

When I first returned to New York from my sojourn in Europe, in the nineteen sixties, I began to meet people more easily and to relate to therm on a new and deeper level. Some of those people I met would end up becoming friends for years, for decades, even for life. Among those I still have contact with of one sort or another with are Jon Petersen and the painter E. Jay Weiss.

Jon lived in the West Village, not far from me; while Jay lived on the Upper East Side. Jay and I were starving artists at the time, but Jon had just produced Israel Horowitz's play *The Indian Wants the Bronx,* an Off-Broadway hit that introduced a new star getting rave notices, Al Pacino, and Jon wasn't suffering financially. Often he'd treat us.

On sunny summer Sundays, we three would meet for brunch at a point midway between our neighborhoods, an open-air cafe located under a huge set of stone steps in Central Park a block or so in, roughly at Seventy-Second Street. It was later closed for years but I hear that it's now been reopened. When it was open during Mayor John Lindsay's administration, it served fairly good, inexpensive meals, and while service could be slow if it was crowded, it had so many tables and was so superlative a people-watching spot that we often didn't mind waiting.

Not only was there good people-watching for those sitting, but also those strolling or gathering at the nearby Bethesda Fountain with its adjacent pond. For a few years in the late Sixties it became an outdoors clubhouse, a weekend meeting place for hip, young New Yorkers, and especially for younger gay men. And as Jay and Jon fit the category and between them seemed to know pretty much everyone I wanted to know, I soon met their friends, and later on ended up at parties and other events with them.

Among that mass of desirable, talented, ambitious young guys were (to me) one particularly golden couple, David Watt and Zeb Freedman. David was tall, fair, with WASPy features and light brown hair. He was solidly built, his body a cross between that of a surfer and a lumberjack. He always looked outdoorsy, out of place in Manhattan, and indeed he relocated to the Hamptons where he began a landscaping outfit that did keep him out-of-doors. I recall seeing David once in Manhattan on a corner of Sheridan Square at midday obviously waiting for someone. He was wearing a T-shirt over what looked like a wet suit, and with his musculature—those thighs!—he was so striking, so out of place, that as I passed, I couldn't help but quip, "Cruising for Orca?"

By contrast, his lover, Zeb, was slender, with dark hair, a Mediterranean complexion that tanned lusciously, and one of those classically handsome Jewish faces that might have come out of an illustrated Pentateuch had such an anomaly existed. In short, he was my absolute archetype—at times my downfall—from junior high school on.

Together, Zeb and David formed a perfection of what I had come to realize was my physical type in men, and in those early years before I came to know either man well, they were for me the *ne plus ultra*. Unsure of myself at the time and of what I believed to be my own very few apparent attractions, I aspired merely to be worthy of existing within their ambit, not even daring to be in their company, though that sometimes did happen.

You can imagine, therefore, my pleasure and surprise when Zeb Freedman phoned me one evening. It was a year or so after the Central Park cafe had closed; Jon and Jay were no longer quite so chummy; I'd not seen the golden couple around in a while—in fact I'd heard that they'd broken up. On the phone, Zeb said he understood I had a young adult, unfixed male cat.

It turned out he had a young adult, unfixed, *female* cat, named Jennie. And at nine months old, Jennie was in heat. *Considerably* in heat, Zeb assured me, keeping him up at night with her meowing and assorted other in-heat noises and gyrations. He'd gotten her only a few months ago, already loved her, and like myself he felt she should not be spayed but should develop "naturally."

He'd not, however, counted on the side effects of that natural upbringing when Jennie reached puberty. While for me, the only problems of leaving Fred unfixed consisted in him trying to spray territorially and his remaining outside at all hours, Jennie was a house cat who did not go out. As a result Zeb's believed she physically suffered. Could he bring Jennie by for Fred to service her?

I'd recently returned to work, clerking at a Doubleday Book Shop, so weekdays were out: we decided upon a Saturday afternoon. Between the evening of the call and the date we had fixed, whenever Fred would come indoors, I'd hug him, groom him, making sure he looked clean and presentable, telling him of his approaching good fortune. I'd already alerted Zeb that while I'd not actually witnessed Fred *in flagrante delecto,* he *had* begun spraying, and from all appearance he seemed well developed and virile. One female cat had tried clmbing into the study window after Fred early one morning, while I was lying in bed reading, and I remember my cat turning on her and hissing her back out. After that, she'd hung around in the yard for hours. I'd assumed she was an *inamorata*. Zeb had agreed that all suggested Fred was sexually active.

I certainly was sexually active, and it wasn't at all difficult in my hormone-drenched mind to construct what would ensue as a result of my offering my cat as a Good Samaritan. Zeb and Jennie would arrive. Fred and Jennie would couple. In gratitude, Zeb would throw himself at me. Then *we* would couple. Jennie would require several, perhaps many, such bouts, week after week, possibly until she conceived. Every time she coupled, so would we. It was a heaven-sent situation. In advance thanks to the spirits, I lit incense and a scented candle.

Zeb came a half hour late, which was fine with me as I had been unexpectedly out late Friday night, and so had awakened late. I was still groggily straightening up the place when he and Jennie arrived. She was inside a handsome cat carrier. Zeb had come from Stuyvesant Town, the planned community across town on the East Side above Fourteenth Street, where he said he was house-sitting his father's flat. Finding the cat carrier and getting a cab had been a hassle.

Zeb still seemed a little flustered. He was tanner than before, handsomer than ever. As he let Jennie out of the carrier to look around the apartment, I invited him to tea and freshly sliced cantaloupe. Fred had gone out earlier, as usual, and hadn't returned. When the bell announcing my visitors rang, I had checked the back yard to see if Fred were nearby, to call him in. No. But he usually came in around noon for lunch. Zeb and I settled in, enjoying the breeze from the back window, eating, drinking, smoking and catching up.

At the time I barely knew him and so could not know, as I later did come to know, that among Zeb Freedman's more unusual characteristics was an breathtaking vagueness about friends and acquaintances and their precise connections, not only to each other, but sometimes also to himself. I could count on one hand the times he and I had met, four times in all: three in Central Park, once at a Jay Weiss party. At each he'd been very much attached to David and we had scarcely spoken.

So you can imagine my wonder when Zeb acted as though we'd known each other all our lives! His style was "natural" in every way: he as easily commented on my taste in music as he did on the freshness of the melon. He sailed into intricate, epic tales of our mutual friend Jay and other people I barely knew, from which it became clear that while Jay thought Zeb his nearest and dearest friend, Zeb himself had serious qualms, never mind intricate criticism. The bloom had not yet left the rose of my own friendship with Jay, although it soon would, so while I listened to Zeb expatiate with some embarrassment, later on I would realize that his assessments and warnings had been both exact and relatively impartial.

I was more than content to feed Zeb, to enjoy his company, to listen to his rich, husky voice, which made him sound as though he was perpetually just recovering from a head cold. I enjoyed his warm, manly, spontaneous laugh. I was happy to share his apparent love of life, and his piercing, if at times off-kilter intelligence which, like a laser with somewhat defective wiring, was able to focus and concentrate—when it did at all— with staggering exactitude.

I'd long admired Zeb's posture, his erect bearing, the way he held himself, and I realized those physiological qualities were reflective of what appeared to be the integrity of his persona. I'd remembered hearing from Jay that Zeb had lived since early childhood with life-threatening diabetes, although to me he'd always seemed more than the picture of health. He now related a few of his more momentous bouts with that illness since childhood, the alarms, the near-deaths, the miraculous revivals—as well as every doctor's unceasingly dark prognostications.

As he spoke, Zeb would alleviate his sober topic with lighthearted asides and generally effervescent spirits. He showed me the palm of his right hand, his lifeline a mere inch from beginning to end: his ostensible future path nought but a blank plain of nearly uninscribed skin—so very different from my own lengthy, irregular, even intermittent, life-line—and he remarked gamely, "That's how long I was *supposed* to live. Less than ten years."

I found myself listening to him with the same attitude that I read a Dickens or Conrad novel: with my fullest attention, enraptured by his victories, captivated by his casual fearlessness. He capped it all by declaring that the disease that everyone from his earliest years on had assumed would define, limit, and constrain his life, hadn't: chiefly because he wouldn't allow it to. I was even more rapt when Zeb then admitted that he knew how sneaky and persistent an illness diabetes was, and he was certain it would one day return in full strength, and in the end maim and kill him, probably before he was forty-five years old.

If I'd felt unequal, inferior to Zeb before that conversation, I also found myself in awe of him. My own problems—poverty, trying to become a writer, getting published—seemed almost inane in comparison to facing death every day as he had to.

Meanwhile, Jennie lurked about the living room and study, sniffing away here and there, doubtless coming upon all kinds of olfactory evidence of my cat. But where was Fred? Zeb and I had eaten the melon and drank a full pot of coffee, and Fred still was nowhere to be seen.

I made futile efforts to search in backyard. I called him. Still no Fred. I was beginning to be embarrassed, even if Zeb was graciousness itself, easily brushing aside my worries: Fred would come, Zeb thought, and all would be well.

Jennie returned to where we sat, and was languidly cleaning herself and allowing herself to be petted. A second later she was transformed into some strange other kind of animal, one I never seen before. She leapt down to the floor, took up a curious squatting position, with her legs bent under her body, her head and tail straight out, her torso rigid, her backside lifted in the air.

I didn't need anyone to tell me that this must be her "in heat" receptive posture. Unbending as she was, she could nevertheless also manage to sidle forward and backward in tiny steps, going nowhere in particular. The upper half of her pretty face seemed to be horizontally distorted, further emphasizing her feline qualities, especially her now slitted eyes, while her lower face seemed pinched in, her teeth set on edge.

Through her rictus, however, she was still able to utter unearthly piercings, less earsplitting than, if identical to, those I'd heard in the middle of the night from other, unseen, cats in the backyard. Jennie was attractive and petite, two-thirds Fred's size, pecan and custard colored, with teak accentuation marks. Suddenly she was utterly grotesque, almost a statue.

Unfazed, Zeb explained what was happening. He removed from her cat carrier a rubber wrapped oral thermometer, and while she stood, rigid, shuddering in place, he gently used it to enter her, to which she responded by backing up into it for more penetration. The sounds she emitted changed from piercing to guttural for a few minutes. He removed it, wiped it with a tissue and put it back into its rubber casing, explaining that my cat's smell must have set off this bout.

He thought that what he'd just done would calm her down. But he added that her in-heat "freezes" were coming far more frequently each day. As though agreeing with Zeb, Jennie altered back from total inflexibility to—in a second—being a playful little cat again. She rolled over onto her back, meowing sweetly, as though asking us to play with her.

During all this, I kept wondering where in the hell Fred was.

One hour turned to two and while I was enjoying myself—Zeb and I hadn't come close to running out of topics to interest us, mostly because it seemed that just about *everything* interested him—I kept worrying when Fred would come home. Jennie went rigid again and Zeb had to service her with the thermometer again, and then yet again. He took it his in stride but I'd definitely begun to feel embarrassed.

At last I heard the familiar thump of Fred landing on the floor inside the study window. As he always did, he announced his presence with meows, then went directly into the kitchen to drink and nibble some food. After that, he came to see who was visiting.

He must have been awfully busy out of doors that day to be so late, and also to be so distracted. It was some time before he smelled Jennie's presence, never mind notice her. He did look great—handsome, masculine, very confident—as he greeted me and Zeb, who was delighted to see him.

Once we'd petted to him and spoken to Fred he turned his attention to where Jennie was sitting in a corner of the living room, from where she had been silently observing Fred's every move since he'd arrived indoors.

I have no idea what I was expecting Fred to do as I'd never seen sexually active cats meet before. I think I expected Fred to act like a young dog first meeting a bitch, to rush over to her and immediately begin sniffing her, as a prelude to unbridled lust.

Instead, Fred looked at Jennie a long while, then he looked at me and began to ask questions, every once in a while looking back at Jennie, but by no means as much as he was looking at me, demanding answers.

It took me a minute to understand that what he wanted to know was who she was and whether she was moving in with us, replacing him, or what? A question any child would ask its parent when placed suddenly in the unexpected presence of another of its kind.

I tried calming Fred, picked him up, held him close to me, although he was big now, not a kitten anymore. In short, I treated him as though he *were* a kitten again—my baby—so he wouldn't feel threatened. Time passed while he settled to sit in my lap, as I continued to reassure him that only *he* counted in my life. Zeb and I discussed what was now unexpectedly happening and he was remarkably patient. Jennie remained seated, unmoving, unchanging.

Who knows how long it was before Fred felt secure again: twenty minutes, a half hour?

All at once, Fred jumped down lightly, took a few steps in Jennie's direction, changed his mind and went back to the kitchen to eat. Who knows what he had decided about the little pecan and custard colored interloper. I shut the window to outside, barring his retreat. He stood in the study there and meowed a few minutes, then seeing he was getting nowhere, he returned to the living room and sat at my feet.

More time went by. Zeb and I got involved in a conversation about parents and how his divorced parents had reacted to his coming out: not great, but not terrible either, given that they were Jewish. During this, Fred got up and walked over to Jennie.

She remained where she was and looked him over. As she'd had several heat attacks already that day, I felt certain she must be putting out all kinds of pheromones, and Fred must be perceiving her existing within a virtual mist of hormonal effusions.

If that was so, Fred didn't let on one bit. He was a very cool customer indeed. Forcing me to wonder exactly how thorough an education in love and romance he'd actually had out in the backyard to be acting so casual around Jennie. He did, at one point, stop at her side, look at us, and ask some question.

"Why isn't he sniffing her?" I futilely asked Zeb. "Why isn't she sniffing him back? Why isn't she in heat, now that she ought to be?"

"God! What a *meshuganah yenta*!" Zeb laughed, using Yiddish for the first time, in effect calling me a crazed matchmaker. "You want a *shaddoch* made in a minute? Maybe they're nervous with us around. Would you want to have sex with people watching?"

Well. . . . I had done exactly that, late last night on one of the mostly enclosed, dilapidated piers once utilized by deluxe ocean liners of the Cunard and White Lines, and now just twisted metal and rotting wood, eroding away a few blocks distant on the edge of the Hudson River. It had been an experience at first so very filled with tension, I'd almost pushed the other guy away from me, and taken off. Luckily, however, he'd been persistent, not to mention accomplished, so I'd accepted his attentions. Then, as the little group gathered around me and my partner of the moment, keeping a distance of a few feet, but also at times reaching out to stroke some exposed part of one of our bodies, whispering instructions or words of encouragement, it had suddenly become very sexy, almost like group sex—or was it more like performance art? Whichever, it had been wonderfully exhilarating. I'd eat ground glass before telling Zeb.

"Why don't we take a walk," he suggested. He was right. It was a beautiful day outside. "And leave them alone to get to know each other."

Fine with me. As we left, Jennie remained sitting where she had been before. Fred had reseated himself precisely where he'd been before, indirectly, ambiguously, facing her. Neither seemed in the least bit interested in each other.

It was a lovely, late spring day, with a fresh strong breeze from the river cooling it off. Zeb confessed to being hungry again, blaming his health condition for the need to constantly stoke up on food. We ended up walking down to Sheridan Square where we had a late lunch in a local cafe recently made famous by Terry Southern in his naughty novel *Candy*. From there we strolled Christopher Street, people-watching, stopping to meet and greet folks, all the way down to the Hudson. It wasn't then as much of a "scene" as it would become in later years for guys to meet, but it seemed that many people we knew happened to be there that lovely Saturday afternoon. We even stopped in a West Street bar for Zeb to use the john, and as the music was good, we danced there a while.

It must have been several hours before we arrived back to my flat. We'd had such a great afternoon, we'd all but forgotten about the cats. But there was Jennie, sitting, although in a new spot, and there, although far away, in fact sitting on my bed in the bedroom, was Fred. Both animals got up to meet their owners. Well, at least they hadn't hurt each other.

But had they done anything else to each other? We couldn't tell.

Zeb tried to see if Jennie had been penetrated, but he had to admit he had no idea how he could be sure. Fred meanwhile walked to the study window, eager to go outside. Both cats seemed extremely matter of fact. We didn't know what to think.

Zeb got Jennie back in the cat carrier with no trouble, and Fred was outside in a sec and we said good-bye. Zeb promised to call and let me know what happened. "Here's hoping!" he said.

Six

Zeb called sometime during the following afternoon to tell me that Jennie had gone into her in-heat "freeze" position three times more since they'd returned home. He wasn't exactly sure whether that meant that she and Fred hadn't mated. He would have to wait and see if it continued, and also check with someone he knew who also had an unfixed female cat.

When Fred stepped in from his outdoor foray an hour later, I called him over, petted him, and tried talking to him about Jennie. I got absolutely nowhere, naturally.

Later that week Zeb phoned and said he'd talked to his woman friend who hadn't been all that clear, but had thought that not sex, but only conception, would end the in-heat cycle Jennie was going through. That, or the cycle would end by itself. By the following Saturday that had not happened, and so Jennie paid another visit in her cat carrier. I'd kept Fred inside since his early lunch, and this time Zeb and I put the two cats together, remained with them, at times physcially pushing their company upon each other.

For at least an hour we tried to get them to at least sit next to each other. Each time Fred would end up wandering off, to nervously nibble at his nearly empty food dish, to scratch himself, to do anything but pay attention to Jennie. This prompted Zeb to wonder if Fred mightn't be, like his owner, not particularly interested in females.

That reminded me of my first roommate, Bobby Brown, who'd moved into this same Jane Street flat several years before while I was unemployed and still recovering from a serious case of mononucleosis. Bobby had brought with him two cats, Speed and Skag, huge, smoke gray brothers born from the same litter, nearly identical.

Although I'd lived in the same apartment with them almost a year, I'd never gotten close to either cat, and they'd pretty much avoided me, except whenever I happened to be feeding them—which was infrequent. In fact, Speed and Skag more or less avoided everyone, including Bobby, preferring to play with, groom, and relate almost exclusively with each other.

Most of the time, they'd be like bookends, sitting or standing about in extremely posed-looking, studio-portrait attitudes. Whenever, however, they did manage to impel themselves or each other into motion, that motion usually consisted of two major types of activity: 1) leaping up against the apartment walls chasing shadows, spiders, poltergeists, hallucinations, or who knew what, and 2) chasing each other around the apartment.

If the first operation was at times bizarre and unnerving, the second could become raucous, and at times downright terrifying. Given the layout of the apartment with its's central wall between the bedroom/bath corridor, living room, study, and kitchen, the cats could manage to chase each other in circles for hours at a time. But sooner or later, one—most often the appropriately named, more indolent Skag—would stop dead. Speed would then appear. Unable to stop himself from his ongoing, headlong rush, Speed would slam into his sibling, resulting in the two of them screeching, hissing, and thumping up against the walls and back down onto the floor. An all-out cat fight would ensue, arousing me from a nap, jarring me from my quiet reading.

But while I sometimes needed a broom to physically separate them, to keep them from killing each other and destroying my home, if he were home and heard them, Bobby would merely sluggishly whine, "Boys! Stop it." Occasionally punctuated with a "Right now!" if they hadn't immediately heeded him.

Despite, or possibly leading up to these fights, was Bobby's unshakeable conviction that Speed and Skag were homosexual lovers. All the affection between them that I'd ever witnessed however was grooming, although I had to admit they did go about it rather more intimately than was common.

Already humiliated for my cat Fred's lack of interest in the lovely Jennie, I came to his defense, decrying Zeb's imputations, naming various female cats I'd seen him with, although if I were sworn to tell the truth, I hadn't a shred of proof he wasn't still as celibate as when I'd gotten him.

Once again, we left Fred and Jennie together for a longish while as we went off to lunch. This time we put them in my bedroom and closed the door on them. Again we went out and had fun, although the weather wasn't as perfect as the previous weekend and I was certain I could hear far less optimistic tones in the subjects Zeb and I spoke of. The instant I cracked open the bedroom door, upon returning home, Fred dashed out of the bedroom, meowing, scratching at the wall, demanding to be let outside.

That Monday evening's report from Zeb was unchanged from before: Jennie was still in heat, though she was acting out far less regularly and less often than before. Perhaps . . . ? We could still hope.

Two months later, Jennie was still not pregnant and was in heat again. Once more Zeb brought her over to visit, and hopefully be made pregnant. But he'd made other plans both weekend days, explaining that family members were in town from the West Coast, and as his father wasn't feeling well, it was Zeb's duty to be with them. He didn't dawdle dropping her off and he collected Jennie quite late both evenings, so casually it was almost as an afterthought. Since the weather was gray and damp and I was busily writing, I remained indoors most of both those days and so could be almost certain that Fred had not done anything toward fulfilling his studly duty.

Embarassed for my cat, feeling guilty, indeed feeling that I had in some crucial way failed Zeb and had already been myself lowered in his eyes, I at last did the only possible noble thing and suggested that he try to locate some other male cat to impregate Jennie.

Had I been able to find out from Fred why he'd avoided Jennie, believe me I would have. He, however, had acted like absolutely nothing was going on. So while I was stumped, and my own lustful plans were utterly destroyed, I shrugged my shoulders, intending to soldier on. I had other more important matters in my life to occupy me.

Writing about this incident at a point in my life some decades along, I'm able to recognize and—without that much rancor—report that my destiny has been an odd one, both in its general contours as well as in its details. One such detail is that I've by now learned that I never get what I want. That is to say, I don't get it *when* I want it. Often, I will get what I want later on. Sometimes so *much* later on I barely recall I ever wanted it. Often, what I wanted has in the meanwhile become tainted or diminished, so that by the time it has come to me, I'm repulsed and push it away. When, that is, I'm not totally indifferent to its sudden, at times awkwardly tardy, arrival.

It's as though I possess an inattentive, even absent-minded, guardian angel who exists in a totally different time-frame, far delayed from my own, who every once in a while suddenly remembers, "Oh wait! Didn't he want that grant?" (Or that award, or that book published, or that recording, or that man in bed.) But not until, say, twenty years after the desire. I have no idea what else could possibly explain the singular, at times understandably frustrating, at times merely baffling, lag between subject and object in my life: I'm merely a reporter and state the facts.

So I can report the fact that it was not for a few years, not till the October of 1973, that I saw Zeb again, one afternoon in San Francisco. I'd flown into the area, and was met at the airport by my pals Arnie and Jan, who were living and working in Big Sur. They'd taken the day off as a holiday and we hung around San Francisco, lunching in Polk Gulch, walking around "Beatsville" (North Beach) spending a few hours in the South of Market gay bathhouse on Ritch Street. I think I might have been delivering something to Zeb from Jay Weiss, and that was how and why I had his address.

He was living on Dolores Street off Eighteenth, in a large, beautifully restored, well-furnished two-story house, along with three other men, one of whom might have been his boyfriend. Zeb looked great, was delighted to see me, and to meet my pals, whom he would later visit at Big Sur often. We had tea and chocolates. He never asked abut my cat and never mentioned his own.

Another five or six years passed before Zeb returned East. This time he phoned me at Fire Island Pines, where since 1975 I'd lived and worked half the year long. Again it may have been Jay or, since we'd fought, maybe Jeannie Owens or even Sam Plaia who'd told Zeb where I was, and he needed to be on Fire Island for some reason or other. Bob Lowe worked weekends, and the other little bedroom was empty, ready for guests, so I invited Zeb to stay as long as he wished.

By then we were in our early thirties, and Zeb was handsomer than ever. He again acted as though we'd never stopped seeing each other, nor being intimate. After the first evening's dinner, and a short, phenomenally romantic, moon and starlit walk to the nearby ocean and back, we ended up in bed together.

During the remainder of that summer Zeb came out whenever the house was otherwise empty and we'd spend time together. Our sexual fit was excellent, and we always had a good time together.

That summer I came to know Zeb better. One time I woke up from an afternoon nap to find him passed out in a diabetic fit. As he'd earlier instructed me in case of just such a mishap, I opened his lips and administered orange juice down his throat, praying he'd live.

He slowly gulped it, swallowed it, and came to. But although we grew close, we never formed a romantic union like the short, tempestuous passions he'd in the years between experienced with my pals Arnie and Jon—and with who knew how many other men.

That summer when I mentioned my interest in his ex-boyfriend of years before, Zeb arranged for me to spend time with David Watt. He was at Fire Island, living in an old house without running water or electricity two towns down the beach at a tiny mid-island hamlet named Onleyville. So—years later—I managed to fulfill that wish too. And as a result of staying with David a few nights, I also meet their pal Steve Lawrence, who owned the funky old house. Steve was a tall, pretty-ugly Texan, a brilliant graphic designer who had begun and published for several years the pathbreaking, all-graphic zine called *Newspaper*. Sometime, later that summer, Steve began visiting me at the Pines and we also became occasional sex-buddies.

When I asked him about Jennie, Zeb admitted he'd tried to get her pregnant again, using another male cat and had failed. Before he moved from Manhattan, he'd given her to a family member who had children, somewhere outside of Manhattan, he was never too clear where, precisely, and I didn't ask.

I'd never truly fathomed Zeb's life, where he was headed, why he did what he did in life or in relationships, so I wasn't overly surprised when he fell out of view after that summer.

He didn't reappear in my life until the late Eighties. People around us then were dying of a brand new epidemic, and Zeb also became ill enough to be hospitalized. At first I thought he too had contracted HIV, but from Jon and a few others who'd remained in better touch with Zeb, I heard that, as he'd foreseen years before, diabetes had at last seized hold of him and was wreaking vengeance for all the fun he'd had and all the off-handed self-care he'd tossed it as a sop.

For all his gallantry, Zeb turned out to be a difficult, unmanageable patient once he was really ill, and what I heard about him, on top of my having to spend time in hospitals with many people far closer to me, meant alas that while I kept intending to, I never saw him again.

I believe Zeb was forty-eight or forty-nine years old when finally he did expire of many depredations particular to that malady, including the loss of a foot and the partial loss of eyesight, as well as multiple cardiac problems. So it was that the intrepid Zeb Freedman nearly quintupled his predicted life span and therefore rather spectacularly swindled the disease. In the process, he made a liar out of dozens of doctors, most of whom were already long gone when he died.

Meanwhile, back in the 1960s, when Zeb temporarily, and Jennie permanently, exited my and Fred's lives I turned back to what I'd been doing before they'd intruded. And I expected Fred would do so too.

It was the same night that I finally gave up and suggested—and Zeb took up the suggestion—that he find some other cat for stud duty. Fred came inside, while I was on the phone, and began sniffing around the spot where Jennie had sat when she was present. This wasn't unusual and I paid little attention to it. I went into the adjacent study to find an address or other piece of information, and remained talking there another fifteen or twenty minutes.

When I brought the phone back to its usual spot, Fred was still sniffing around the floor near my knock-off bentwood rocking chair. And he was talking, asking questions. I assumed about Jennie and so I replied that she was gone. Gone home. Gone for good. Never to return. I didn't blame him. I was merely letting him know.

Fred continued to sniff and meow around that spot. I tried holding and petting him, re-explaining what had happened. He squirmed out of my arms, returning to the rocker and continued to meow. I ignored him and went to make dinner.

When I brought my food out to the table. Fred hadn't moved from the rocker. In fact now he was sitting exactly where Jennie had sat all those previous times she'd visited. I went over to him and tried explaining to Fred that she was gone. Kaput. Forever. He wasn't getting it.

That night, he didn't come and lie down on the little oval carpet next to my bed, but remained at the spot in the living room near the rocking chair. I know because I saw him there when I got up to use the john during the night. I tried to carry him into the bedroom, nuzzled his face, set him down on the rug. A minute later he'd fled and when I got up to check, he was in the living room and—you guessed it—sitting by the rocking chair again.

He was there the next morning too. In fact, he wouldn't leave the spot except to come and meow plaintively at me while I was drinking my morning coffee and reading the newspaper. He did briefly run to the kitchen when I opened a new can of wet food for him, but once the food was on the plate, he merely sniffed at it, and didn't take a bite.

It was a lovely morning and I opened the study window, thinking he'd as usual, go outside while I settled in at my desk and wrote. An hour later, when I got up to check a spelling in a dictionary, Fred was still sitting by the rocker. He continued to whine at me. I picked him up and put him on the study windowsill, pushing him outside. He turned around and came back in and ended up back at the rocker.

Fred's vigil continued all day. He refused to eat. He may have swiped a little water out of his bowl, but not any noticeable amount. Every once in a while, he'd stand up and begin sniffing around, concentrating on the spot where Jennie had sat on her five visits, but also at other spots around the living room I remembered seeing her in. Wherever I went, he'd follow me around, meowing questions, sounding at once both pathetic and accusatory. He refused to go outside.

Once when I got up from my work and went to get something out of the kitchen, I caught Fred in the bedroom, standing on his hind legs and using his front paws to knead at the chenille bedspread where I recall having seen Jennie sitting when we'd locked the two cats together in my bedroom. He'd never done that before.

"Stop! You'll rip my spread!"

When he didn't stop I pulled him away and out of the room. He batted me back, and struck out at me. A first. He hissed at me. Another first. He ran out into the living room, and whenever I tried to get near him, he would rear up on his hind legs, try to strike me, and hiss.

"What's gotten into you?" I asked.

But I already knew. Or at least suspected I knew.

I avoided him all the rest of the day and wrapped his food with plastic wrap and refrigerated it for the following day. Fred kept to his vigil at the rocking chair.

The next day was just the same: without food, and it seemed also without sleep, Fred had become almost unmanageable. I couldn't even get near the rocker without his lashing out at me. And I had to keep the bedroom door closed. Finally, he hissed at me once too often, and managed to scratch me—an unthinkable breach of our affection. I picked him up roughly and tossed him out the study window and slammed it shut.

Fred remained outside at the windowsill all the rest of the evening, scratching at the window, and meowing. At nine o'clock I got a phone call from the woman who lived in the back part of the apartment on the left of me. She was an actress, unmarried or long divorced, in her mid-fifties by that time, once good looking if never stunning, somewhat blowsy, a bit of drinker, whom I'd occasionally witnessed dragging home drunker, usually younger men, from the bar and hamburger joint on the corner of Jane and West Fourth Streets. She still occasionally showed up in minor parts in Off-Broadway plays. Her greatest success had been a five minute speaking part, as a worried waitresss in a beseiged restaurant, in one of Hitchcock's best movies, *The Birds*.

She kept a small and quite perfumed pug dog and an elderly, unfriendly Burmese cat in her tiny, lower floor, back apartment and she was familiar with all the local cats (including mine), some of whom she had nursed and fed after fights. She phoned me that evening to tell me that Fred was outside and was— uncharacteristically—making a nusiance of himself, meowing at my study window, and also down, outside her bedroom window.

I apologized and explained to her what had happened.

"No wonder!" she replied. "He's in love."

Much as I valued Fred, I considered ascribing human emotions to animals foolish. So naturally I downplayed it.

After I'd hung up the phone. I opened the study window and pulled Fred inside. He made a pest of himself that night and I ended up sleeping with ear plugs, since he seemed intent on keeping me awake.

The next morning however my patience was at an end, and Fred and I ended up having our first (and it turned out last) real fight. He scratched me badly along the arm and I threw him across the room, then charged angrily after him. He managed to elude me and scrambled out the study window and out of sight in the back yard.

Fred remained outside for the next two days and nights, and I received no phone calls about him meowing at Grace's window. Luckily for him, as I was by this time deeply pissed off.

Fred wasn't stupid, and when he next showed up, it was with full knowledge of how bad his behavior had been. He waited a full day after I'd once more reopened the study window, in effect reinviting him back in. When he showed up, he sat on the wndow sill without coming in, almost without moving, checking me over for at least two hours while I ate dinner and read. I ignored him. Finally, when I was ready to go to bed, I put out a tentative hand in truce. He sniffed it, nuzzled it, and typical of Fred and no other cat I've ever known, he laid his own left paw upon it, while looking at my face. Shaking my hand—establishing a truce.

"Okay, then, Come on in!" I petted his head, and he leapt inside.

He ate all the dinner I'd saved for him. And while he came into my bedroom to sleep as he used to do, upon the little rug next to my bed, from which he could stand up and nuzzle me while I slept, he did go back out into the living room, where he ended up sleeping next to the rocking chair.

Without Fred around to irritate me over those few days, I'd given much thought to his plight. While I didn't at all go along with Grace about Fred falling in love, I realized that some kind of attachment had been formed by Fred with Jennie. I tried to reconstruct events and to understand them from his point of view.

At first, Fred had been trespassed upon—his space, his territory, his human friend—by this other cat, someone he'd never seen before. She'd turned out not to be quite the invader he at first thought, vanishing two nights in a row. Then she'd vanished for a week, and then for two entire months.

She had been sweet tempered, and easy-going. She smelled all right. She didn't eat out of his dish or drink out of his water bowl. When they'd been locked together in the bedroom, she'd probably not been demanding or complaining. Perhaps they'd gotten friendly—in a way. Perhaps she'd progressed from fear and uncertainty to being open to being sniffed by him.

We already knew they had not had sex, and perhaps my own training of Fred, little as that was, was partly responsible for that fact. I'd trained him not to spray inside the apartment. Therefore Fred probably assumed that the apartment was not part of his sexual territory. Maybe he thought it was my sexual territory—which it was. Or off-limits to all cats.

So when Zeb and I tried to get him to perform sexually inside the house, Fred was confused. It was like asking Christians to have sex in church. Not only was it not done, but if it were done, it could be pretty uncomfortable too. Sex was for the backyard. For outside. Period. Even so, Fred had perhaps come to like Jennie, and once she was totally withdrawn from his life, he wanted to know why. He missed her.

The rest was all miscommunication between me and Fred.

Once I had gotten that far in my thinking, I began to feel remorse for how I'd unthinkingly mistreated Fred. I tried to make it up to him, but how? He was too old for toys. Food treats were possible but insignificant. All I could do was love him.

I promised myself I would do that as well as I could and especially I would respect him as a cat. I'd never again befuddle him by crossing what for him must be very important and distinctive signals. I'd never expect him to be anyone other than who he already was.

After a few weeks, Fred and I settled back into our relationship. He never quite forgot Jennie however, because he took up her sitting spot at the rocking chair as his favorite spot indoors thereafter, a sort of homage to her, I came to believe.

And while we were friends again, it was also true that we no longer possessed the kind of easy affability with each other we once had. Fred would stay out of doors for longer periods of time, until keeping food and water dishes out for him only seemed to interest cockroaches. He slept inside often, drank out of the toilet, and I'd feed him whenever I did see him. But Grace would report not seeing him in the back yard, but instead in front, on Jane Street, once outside the Eclair Factory, alongside the big yellow tomcat he'd once fought with, old enemies turned pals.

My own life became filled with dance, music, men, drugs, parties, and fun. I began going out to Fire Island at this time, at first for weekends at a time, then for weeks, finally for entire summers, and I always kept the window open a crack, just enough for Fred to sidle into. When I began going away whole summers, I sublet the apartment to a friend, and Joe claimed he got along well with my cat.

Fred always did seem happy to see me when I returned in October. But after a few days of hanging around indoors, Fred would once more be off on two- and three-day jaunts. Once, past midnight, in late February, with freezing temperatures and light dusting of snow on the ground, as I was stepping out of a taxicab on Houston Street at Broadway, along with two friends, headed toward Flamingo, our favorite dance club, I thought I saw Fred on the sidewlak.

"Fred—dd?" I called.

He turned and came over to me. Sure enough it was him.

He was a mile and a half, and several major urban avenues from where I lived. He stuck around just long enough to be petted by my companions, then took off, after who knew what Saturday night fun, while I—shaking my head in wonder—did the same.

Inevitably, the day arrived when Fred didn't come home at all. At least a week had passed. Too long for him.

I found an old photo and began making up my own sign for a missing cat. I put it up on every light pole within a three block radius.

That evening I received a phone call from Mizz Chavis-Wilson. She hadn't seen Freddie in days, she told me. I told her he'd been gone a week. She said she would find out if any of his other "regulars" had seen him.

The next day she called on me in person. With her was Mrs. Ventador, another of "Silver's" regulars. Grimly they reported that no one among the cat ladies had seen Fred in at least five days. They would continue to ask around, however. I wasn't to lose hope. Fred might have been taken indoors by someone who didn't know he was free and he might not be able to get out again.

When I told them about seeing Fred a mile and a half away, Mizz Chavis-Wilson put a hand up to her mouth in shock. More stoic, Mrs. Ventadorn shook her head. "Giving freedom to a pet also means having to give him up for good if need be."

It was Mrs. Ventadorn who phoned me two days later to tell me that the women on Horatio Street had planned a gathering, to include a seance. They would discover, once and for all, just where Fred was.

By then, however, I already believed I knew where he was: run down crossing the six lanes of Houston Street or Sixth Avenue. His body kicked aside, or swept up into a trash bin. He was gone.

It was a month before I heard anything from the Horatio Street cat ladies. By then, most of my notices about Fred had shredded in the late spring winds or been soaked through by hard rains, or tore themselves off light poles. I came upon Mizz Chavis-Wilson across the street. She was holding a tiny little black kitten with white throat bib and mittens, taking it from a neighbor across the street whose cat had had a litter.

Mizz Chavis-Wilson avoided me, so I followed her and had to keep asking what had happened at the seance, before she finally turned to me and shook her head. When I tried to question her more, she held out the kitten to me. But though it was cute as could be, it was my turn to shake my head and push it aside. She nodded her nearly skull-like head at that gesture; she knew Fred could never be replaced that easily, never mind so easily forgotten.

I sulked all the rest of that day, remembering my cat, my buddy, whom I'd raised, all the good times we'd had together, from the day he arrived home a tiny kitten demanding to sleep right next to me on my bed, wrapped in a towel, I recalled everything, even the few bad times, especially the three days when he'd come home stealthily and he'd stayed hidden in my closet, recovering from a bad cat fight where he'd been bitten and trounced. And of course, I couldn't forget the one time Fred and I had fought, because of Jennie.

Seven

There would be other cats in my life after Fred had vanished and Mizz Chavis-Wilson, Grace, Mrs. Ventadorn and the others had assembled to locate him and had instead discovered him among the spirits of the afterlife. The first new cat showed up a few years after Fred was gone, only six months after I moved into my new digs, my first change of apartments in a decade.

With the success of my first two books, and especially the paperback of *Eyes,* a large initial advance was in store for the next novel, *The Mesmerist.* Substantially larger, so that when my accountant heard about it, he immediately set up an I.R.A. plan for me, began discussing investments I ought to be making and set me up to meet with an investment counselor he knew. He also told me that if I wanted to move into more expensive digs, this was the time to do so.

One quarter to one third of my new rent and utilities, as well as all new office furnishings would be tax deductible. It was clear to him that I needed both a new place to live in, one with a real study, as well a place to serve as the main office of my new small press publishing company, the SeaHorse Press. He assured me that I ought to think of whatever rent I would pay out each month, *less* the amount of the tax deduction. Thus I could easily afford a larger, new place.

That summer of 1977, I'd begun work on a new title, *The Lure,* but I'd stopped about a hundred manuscript pages in, realizing I needed far more research before I could continue. With *The Mesmerist,* set in Nebraska Territory at the turn of the twentieth century, all my research could be handled through letters, by telephone calls and in reference libraries reading through journals, letters and newspapers. But aside from Arthur Bell's few, pathbreaking articles in *The Village Voice* that had kicked off my interest in the subject of the new novel, no reference works existed documenting the underground after-hours gay scene I hoped to portray. I'd have to go into that world myself.

I set aside the winter of 1977–1978 to do so, and was helped along when Bob Lowe, the person closest to me, was offered and took a job four nights a week, including weekends, as head barkeep at a club named the Cock-Ring that had opened earlier that year on Christopher

Street and the Hudson River, and quickly become the hottest club on the scene. That autumn, as Bob entered more deeply the world of gay bars and clubs, so did I. By the end of that winter, how dangerous that world could be was made apparent, when three men closing out the cash registers of another club that Bob sometimes subbed in were robbed at gunpoint, shot and left for dead. Only one survived.

During that summer, I had made the big decision to move. In mid-September, as soon as temperatures began to drop, I'd returned from Fire Island to Manhattan and gone through the Sunday *New York Times,* looking for a new place.

I'd been paying $181.00 a month for my little Jane Street place, rent-controlled of course. Looking at ads, I already could tell that if I wanted to remain in the West Village and find something more spacious, I'd have to pay a thousand dollars a month. Suddenly possessing an income many times that, it didn't seem like too much. So I looked for what were called "luxury" apartments.

Four were listed in my neighborhood, and I set myself up to see all four the following day. The first was a flat of six rooms on 11th Street off Sixth Avenue, laid out more like those in San Francisco than New York. It was a lovely area, and the handsome, bright, apartment on the fifth floor had many windows, high ceilings, nineteenth-century touches like crown moldings, fireplaces, and two bay windows. Near subways, shopping and bus lines, its drawback was that it overlooked an old Jewish cemetery, which although it was a historical monument, still gave me the creeps.

The second apartment was already taken when I arrived. I never even looked at it. The third was on Eighth Avenue and Twelfth Street, in the tall, elegant, doorman building above my little Chase bank branch. A top floor, it had stupendous views of the city from front and back windows and a sunken living room. But the bedroom was small and the office even smaller. Later on I saw it furnished when I visited a porn star, Casey Donovan, who'd taken it.

The third place I looked at that day was in an 1839 building, one of two attached four-story structures fronted by a courtyard containing an English Plane tree, wrapped by a wrought iron fence and gate. Quieter than the other two, as it was further west, it was a long, narrow duplex: upper high-ceilinged floor with entry, bath, two fireplaces and eight-foot sliding doors between the office and living room; the downstairs low-ceilinged with a kitchenette, cozy if large dining room and good sized front bedroom. It boasted two full baths and more than adequate storage space: I could see being both a writer and small press publisher there. I liked it instantly. Too instantly, so I phoned Bob as soon as I got home and asked him to come look at it the next day. He liked it as much as I did and I signed a lease.

Among all my residences, only comparable in charm and attractions to the little California house I now live in, the Eleventh Street duplex was my favorite apartment. I remained thirteen and a half years and I'd be there today if not for circumstances beyond my control.

Six months after I'd moved in, I found a good looking young gay carpenter and had him design and build bookshelves into the library on either side of the fireplace. I had another friend of a friend rebuild, restuff, and reupholster the huge old palm fan mahogany Biedermeier era sofa that had been erected and left over a century in the flat. I bought new furniture, Tabriz carpets and reframed art, selling or giving away most of my Jane Street furniture, including the church pew. From one Fire Island friend I bought a sleigh bed the age of the building, and from sometime lover Hal Seidman, I bought a double mattress that fit the frame perfectly, receiving as a bonus Yves St. Laurent sheets and a down quilt I still own. Another bonus was the threeway, Hal, Jim and I had on the new bed the afternoon I received it.

One afternoon, months after I'd settled into the place, I looked up from work at my spiffy new Sloan's reproduction Queen Anne desk in my front office to hear a familiar thump on the wooden floor forty-five-feet away in the living room. A minute later I observed a blue-gray, longhaired Persian cat carefully, confidently, weaving around the furniture to come pay me a visit.

I petted her and asked where she came from. She gazed up at me with her curiously squashed little face and large bittersweet chocolate eyes, and walked back and forth, caressing my hand and wrist with her ultra-soft, luxurious fur. She never meowed. Not then nor later. And I don't think I ever saw her hiss. I did once see her run. But as a rule, she walked, or rather glided, like a runway model or a cruise-liner being tugged to its berth from a long jaunt on the Caribbean.

I have no idea where the Persian came from. I asked around the neighborhood, including the cat ladies of Jane Street, only four blocks away. I put up signs for a few weeks but no one ever responded. Could she have been left there? Dropped off from a passing car on Greenwich Street? No one ever knew, or if they did, never said.

She had come in through the living room window, left open and as a rule unscreened in the early part of spring. The window was seven feet above the sidewalk, guarded by wrought iron gratings. But that hadn't seemed to matter to her in the least, unathletic as she later proved to be. I assumed she leapt up to the window sill from the mesh metal cage puffed over one dining room window below. But I might be wrong: she could have been placed there by an unseen hand.

My friend Jerry Blatt was at that time back in New York, having fought badly with his partner, Bette Midler, and he was working with a new chanteuse. Tally Brown was a heavy-set, heavily cosmeticized, underground "star" who'd been in a few underground (i.e., independent) movies and who was interested in putting together a unique night club act. It was Jerry, the second he saw my new cat, who immediately dubbed her "Tally," probably because she and the chanteuse shared a quiet dignity, bulbous shape, flat leonine face, and long, wild mane of hair. But as the Persian settled in living with me and I came to understand her disposition better, the name Tally altered, simplified, made far more apt, as "Miss Cat."

My last cat experience had been Fred, the most candid, the most masculine of felines. By our last months together, he'd required virtually no care. It seems that everyone in the neighborhood vied to feed him and put him up when I wasn't available. This cat, exactly to the contrary, being a "Blue Point Angora" according a book on cats I bought (felt I *must* buy, *must* read such a book), required *immense* amounts of care.

First, she needed a cat box, and so one was purchased: the best, naturally, since now I could afford it, with the newest brand of deodorized litter. I set up the kit first in the downstairs bathroom, then, when she proved to be a slovenly box-cat, I moved it beneath a turn-of-the-century fainting sofa, in a little used corner of the downstairs dining room.

Second, because she was after all long-haired, she required biweekly combing, brushing, and on top of that regular shampooing. In addition, she needed twice a week eggs and frequent olive oil mixed into her food to maintain the resplendence, softness and sheen of her hair. People who knew cat breeds said she was choice, a purebred, I'd should enter her into a show. Sure.

I should have, given what I'd begun to spend on her. Whereas Fred would eat leftover pasta—let's face it, he'd eat leftover *anything*—Miss Cat required food in tins, or out of little plastic packets: liver pate, whitefish, occasionally a packet of cut-up steak. Heaven forbid I had nothing left in the house but tuna or sardines! She'd nibble at them just enough to show me she flatly refused to go hungry, but she would end up leaving the bulk. Had she been around when I first got Fred, she would have starved to death—and looked terrible.

But her timing had been great and so Miss Cat looked—well, she looked simply *fab-u-lous!* And what was worse, somehow or other she seemed to know it. I write that with some amazement because again, totally the opposite of Fred, she wasn't particularly intelligent. In fact, after a few years I decided that only a tiny, scarcely folded, quite dim little brain existed deep behind her adorable pug face. It made little sense to expect anything special from her mentally: she would as soon open a door with her paws as she would sprout wings and fly, and sitting on the toilet like Fred in imitation of me? Come on now! Miss Cat would solve Fermat's Theorem more quickly! No, she was just intelligent enough to survive—and prosper.

And she was vain. So *very* vain. Long before Carly Simon sang the song, Miss Cat was it's subject—its apotheosis.

I had placed a rectangular, wood-framed mirror upon the living room fireplace mantel, where it might reflect art and open up all that white space. Within a day of her relocating herself into my home and life, Miss Cat decided *that* would become her roost. I had two pale-blue lustrework candlesticks on the mantel and when she first leapt up, I tried her shoo her away, fearing she would break them. Delicate and agile, despite the half-foot of encircling fluff, Miss Cat politely declined to be removed, thank you very much. And she appeared irritated that I'd ever dreamed she would be gauche enough to threaten the candlesticks—which after all, in proximity to her would really bring out those cerulean tints.

Thereafter, she remained on the living room mantel for hours at a time, far happier now that she had a view of things, more content than when she was lying, legs spread out upon my expensive, handsome, also matching, freshly cleaned carpets; blither than she was upon the wide-beamed, original wooden floor, highly polished every week by the cleaning lady; more content even than when she was perched on her second favorite spot, the satiny new pale gold material of the refinished antique sofa.

It didn't take me that long to figure out why Miss Cat loved the mantel spot so much: from there she might uninterruptedly, troublelessly, freely gaze upon her reflection in the mirror.

Miss Cat loved looking at herself in the mirror. She also loved being adored by others. Whenever company arrived and naturally after a few minutes found themselves seated in the living room, she would suddenly drop down from her mirrored throne and deign to meet the guests. All but the most ailurophobic would immediately ooh and ahh, and pet her, commenting on how beautiful she was, how soft her hair was, how gentle a being she was.

Her grace and attraction having been commented upon, her ego once more firmly reinvigorated, Miss Cat would effortlessly ascend to the fireplace mantel and sit for hours in grateful appreciation of a life of such ease and cultivation.

Bob and I sometimes speculated that she was a Yellow Book aesthete reincarnated: Walter Pater or Aubrey Beardsley. I almost called her Aubrey, until I discovered under all that fluff the unmistakable, nearly nonexistent, emblem of her female gender.

Like my first cat, Gustave, Miss Cat did little or nothing of interest in life except exist. Unlike him, her sweetness of disposition was closely allied to her narcissism, which meant she was never for an instant self-effacing. But again, like Gustave, the way she took her leave of my life was also bizarre, if somewhat less sensational and unquestionably less conclusive.

With the publication of *The Lure* in the fall of 1979, a few years after Miss Cat entered my life, I'd embarked upon my first, wildly successful, national book tour, to Boston, Philadelphia, Chicago, San Francisco and Los Angeles. At my insistence, Bob stayed at my place much of that time, as he was still living with, if not on the best terms with, Rodney Bennett, his ex-boyfriend, then head choreographer of the Pennsylvania Ballet, with whom he'd broken up several years before.

Two years later, when my next, also gay-themed novel, *Late in the Season,* came out, I went on another book tour. Sporadically during that year I was out of town at lit conferences, guest teaching and guest lecturing. Bob didn't always stay at my place the times I was away, but he did always drop in to feed and pet Miss Cat.

It was after a later work-related journey that I returned home to find Miss Cat gone, vanished back out the same window through which she'd entered my life. Her food was uneaten, her catbox unused. But her thorough loathing of me for having had the extreme bad taste to desert her was made manifest by the presence in my upstairs bathtub of two reproachful turds, neatly placed, side by side.

I supposed at the time that Miss Cat had moved on to a fresh new duplex or townhouse where she would be more actively, more slavishly admired. My life at the time was quite crowded with writing, small press publishing and my growing affection for Bob, so I have to admit I scarcely missed her.

A few years later, I received, and redelivered by hand to someone four doors down Greenwich Street a piece of important-looking personal mail that had been misdelivered to me—and there was Miss Cat! She was perched in all her vapid magnificence upon a mahogany Victorian plant stand from which all inkling of botanical origins had been effaced. She was purring away, and I must say, she looked smashing, better groomed than I'd ever been able to keep her. I petted her, and she even half stood to receive my caresses. But suddenly, right in the middle of our re-encounter, she bluntly turned her backside to me, and flipped up her bushy tail, pretending not to know who I was, and—evidently still offended by my untasteful desertion—she leapt away, swinging her angora hips off to the kitchen without so much as a glance back.

Her new owner, a middle aged ceramist, wondered aloud at her behavior. "Well, I'll be, " she said. "Missy," she assured me, "is usually *such* a little lady!"

A few years later, I was living half the year at Fire Island Pines when my last live-in cat entered my life. Bob would come out to the Pines on weekends and whenever he had a break from work. But he'd at last moved out of Rodney's Upper West Side flat and into his own place, a tiny, long, third-floor, one bedroom place on Horatio Street, a few blocks from me. There he installed his bed, a kitchen set I provided, his desk and chair, his stereo equipment, his many recordings and books—and his cat, by then almost twelve years old and named Max . . . You Sly Puss.

The name of course was Bette Davis's greeting to George Saunders in the brilliant film, *All About Eve*. And as Max was born into a theatrical world and lived within a theatrical world, the name stuck. Even when it was shortened to simply Max dot dot dot.

I can't recall what reason Bob gave for moving Max . . . out to the Pines with me, but I said sure. I didn't much remember Max . . . except that he was a big, neutered, yet not at all overweight cat with Siamese features, suggesting he was a cross between that breed and a tabby. Many people of course are nuts about full bred Siamese, and I've met maybe one I could actually tolerate. But there's no doubt that their coloring and markings are gorgeous.

Basically a wan gray that shone as pale gold in some lights, Max . . . had a Siamese's dark coloring on his head and shoulders, his underbody, feet, and paws. Also he had a dark thick line along the spine right out to the end of his tail. But his facial and body features were far less bony and starving-model than a purebred. It was a fascinating combination, and standing still or in motion, he was a beauty.

Max . . . was undoubtedly a housecat. He'd never been outdoors except one time when he'd run away and had been found shivering in the large, damp, mazelike corridors of Bob and Rodney's building's basement and laundry room. He arrived at Fire Island with Bob in a meshwork catcage, from which he peered with enormous interest. He never lost the interest in his surroundings, and his intelligence—while never as practical as Fred's—was both obvious, and directly attached to his abiding curiosity, making Max . . . a good deal more interesting to watch and live with than I'd at first anticipated.

Once inside the little oceanside Tarpon Walk house, Max . . . remained indoors. He never once ventured outdoors, even though we were in and out a hundred times a day, and virtually lived out on the three breezy decks that trebled the living area of the tiny house.

Perhaps Max . . . never left because he could see what was going on quite well from inside: through the full length screen doors, kept open and unlatched day—and if it was warm out, all night too; through the living room's catty-corner picture windows, only a foot off the floor, upon which he'd raise himself on his back legs to stare hours at a time; through the back and side windows of the little dining room, with handy shelving upon which he'd perch to gaze out of doors; and through either bedroom window with a chest of drawers considerately drawn up as stepladder and roosts for him to observe from.

Birds mostly were what Max . . . observed with such intensity and fortitude. Fire Island Pines is a federal and state park as well as a bird sanctuary, and birds flocked to the place and lived there in the thousands. Even exposed as the little house was, it attracted birds to the surrounding chokecherry bushes we made sure were kept grown over six feet high for privacy on two sides. Birds lived there, nested there, hunted insects there, ate fruit there—and also upon the surrounding wooden deck. And Max . . . was totally fascinated by birds.

But what also kept Max . . . indoors was fear. Even when I tried dragging him out, feet first out the back screen door onto the deck for some fresh air, he'd scramble like a panicked thing, and wouldn't be content until he was let back inside

As though to mock his fears, fate had managed to place Max . . . at a site where the incessant, vagrant, utterly unpredictable maritime winds would constantly keep him on his toes. Because of all the cross currents running through the little house, any item not itself dense or weighted down might take flight at any second.

Because of the house's height and prominence at the top of the walk's highest natural elevation, we found it perfect for flying kites. We'd pull kites out of bedroom shelf storage and simply attach them by a string to the flagpole, then toss them into the air as high as we could. They would catch a draft of air, and remain fluttering noisily above us days at a time.

My own new kite that year was a bat, in honor of *Die Fledermaus*. It was a charcoal gray, silken, wide triangular object, with bright black and yellow eyes painted close to its central bar. I generally kept it stuffed in the four inch space made by a slightly dropped structural ceiling beam that separated the dining room from the living room.

Bob and I were sitting at the dining room table, having just finished a repast. It was still light out of doors, although past sunset, and the winds had been ceaselessly toying with magazines, the table linen, my writing paper, any object light enough to take flight. Max . . . had been at the house all summer and had become inured to it somewhat, though he'd still not quite lost his general skittishness.

That evening however, he'd found himself chasing a large variety of objects, pillow tassels, sheets of paper, sent into motion by the wayward winds blowing through the house. He was jumpy and on edge. When Bob arrived from the city earlier that evening, Max . . . and Bob had their usual roughhouse greeting-dispute, which also served to keep Max . . . on edge. He'd at last crept out of his usual hiding spot under our bed, come out into the living room, and meowed something, to which Bob responded testily, "Sure. Sure. Sure. We know!"

Max . . . was not impressed by the answer. He meowed back, clearly daring Bob. Then stopped where he stood and began to clean himself. A sudden gust of wind entered the house from behind us, and was angled upward by the intervening dining table. It managed to shove my bat kite out of its perch.

Max . . . looked up, just in time to see this large-eyed monster charge down at him. Who knew exactly what terror he experienced at that moment. He leapt up in the air and out of its path. It sailed on past him, crashing into the living room picture window. Max . . . meanwhile leapt maybe three feet into the air, he landed, immediately scrambled along the wooden floor, headed toward the bedroom, his safety spot. But just as he reached the doorway, the wind slammed the bedroom door in his face with a great boom. Max . . . shot back into the air with a screech, all of his fur sticking straight out. He landed again and turned toward the other bedroom doorway, only to have *that* door suddenly slam into his face. He gave the most unearthly shriek I've ever heard, and dashed around the house, utterly unhinged. He finally found a hiding spot, deep between the two love seats in the living room.

Max . . . didn't come out for two days, no matter how much we coaxed him, and finally Bob had to move his food and water dishes under there so Max . . . wouldn't starve. I am not embarassed to relate that Bob and I laughed long and hard over poor Max . . .'s terri-flying experience.

As you might have ascertained, Max . . . wasn't really my kind of cat. But as we were thrown together alone so much, we ended up becoming friendly, if never as close as Fred and me. He spent three summers living with me but he seemed to forget who I was whenever he returned to the city in autumn. He lived to be fourteen years old, and the night Max . . . died, even though he'd been evidently failing for weeks and had altogether stopped eating or drinking water, Bob was so distraught, he cried himself to sleep in my arms.

Since Max . . . other cats have appeared in my life, for a few days at a time, as I visit where they live, like the Maine Coon cats Blanche and Stella who reside amid quite good Stickley furniture on Manhattan's West End Avenue, or the all white, one long-haired, one short-haired Atwater Village cats, Squeaky and Smudgy, whom I see maybe once a month.

Only lately, an all black, young adult female cat has made an appearance in my life. Similar to the very first cat I can remember, my mother's pet, Chloe, this one is slender, slinky, and so elusive that I've not been able to get close enough to her to read her name tag. She moved in with the couple who took over the rehabbed three-story house one address up the hill from me. As they possess little actual land on their property— though they have a most magnificent series of views— the cat has naturally enough taken to dropping down along the steeply angled, ivy-covered slope to hang out every other day or so upon the more horizontal levels of the three terraces comprising my house's surroundings.

She looks to be about a year old, but I can't tell if she's fixed or not. She's very well cared for, well fed and exercised, and quite sleekly beautiful. I've found her sitting in various spots around the decks. I've watched her tightrope walking along the half-inch-wide top of the six-foot-high fence. I've seen saw her lying in wait for one of the many pigeons, ring doves, secretary birds, finches, California bluejays, yellow orioles, and hummingbirds that crowd the rich native and imported foliage. I've come upon her hunched over, her attention focused upon four-inch-long lizards in my upper garden, and I've witnessed her pawing fascinated at gopher holes she can't get into.

She is very shy, very skittish, and I'm guessing she's originally an apartment cat, only let out a few hours at a time. My landlord hates her, and speaks poorly of her, although I've not seen her doing anything bad. He's a good man and an intelligent one, so I have to wonder if he isn't reacting to her color, and to many people's ingrained fear and abhorrence based on superstition.

Just a few days ago, she was sitting much closer to where I read magazines midday out on the middle terrace, and when I said hello to her, she blinked both her eyes at once, the way that cats do to show that they've heard you, recognized you and decided to respond.

It's a small gesture, but a real one. And while I know she'll never be as deeply connected or loving or trusting, or at times as baffling and misunderstanding as my all-time favorite cat Fred, or indeed any of the other cats I've lived with and grown fond of, I feel certain that in time she and I will become friends.